WHO KILLED ART DECO?

CHUCK BARRIS

SIMON & SCHUSTER PAPERBACKS

NEW YORK   LONDON   TORONTO   SYDNEY

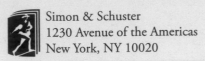

Simon & Schuster
1230 Avenue of the Americas
New York, NY 10020

First Simon & Schuster trade paperback edition June 2009

SIMON & SCHUSTER and colophon are registered trademarks of Simon & Schuster, Inc.

For information about special discounts for bulk purchases, please contact Simon & Schuster Special Sales at 1-800-456-6798 or business@simonandschuster.com

The Simon & Schuster Speakers Bureau can bring authors to your live event. For more information or to book an event contact the Simon & Schuster Speakers Bureau at 866-248-3049 or visit our website at www.simonspeakers.com.

Designed by Nancy Singer

Manufactured in the United States of America

10 9 8 7 6 5 4 3 2 1

Library of Congress Cataloging-in-Publication Data

Barris, Chuck.
  Who killed Art Deco? : a novel / Chuck Barris.
     p. cm.
  1. Adult children—Crimes against—Fiction. 2. Rich people—Fiction.
3. Kentucky—Fiction. I. Title.
  PS3552.A7367W46 2009
  813'.54—dc22
                                          2008032377
ISBN: 978-1-4165-7559-7

FOR MARY

Contents

LIFE CHANGES, DON'T IT?

Eddie Cotton

WHO KILLED
ART
DECO?

ONE

THE
VICTIM

I

Arthur Deco Junior was behaving like Euro-trash.

He was spending his trust fund on drugs and drink, cavorting with weird, freaky friends, and wearing bizarre clothes. Art Deco had let his hair grow down to his shoulders. He wore an earring in one ear. Strange objects dangled from his neck. He had put on weight. He looked nothing like his original self. Friends of his family had no idea who Arthur Deco Junior was when they passed him on the street in New York, and therefore didn't report his bizarre behavior to his father in Bowling Green, Kentucky.

Art roamed all over the East Village with half-wit friends until the wee hours of the morning, zonked out of his mind on alcohol, assorted narcotics, and hallucinogens inhaled, injected, taken down the throat, and up the ass. When the evening had finally gone belly-up, the drugged heir to a monstrous Kentucky fortune would hitch a ride back to his Park Avenue duplex apartment with the first available garbage truck going his way. The workers of the New York Sanitation Department's midnight-to-eight shift knew Arthur Deco Junior well. They referred to him as Young Artie.

Junior was living an existential life. Or trying to. He was attempting to exist in the moment and to the max. It was the popular thing to do among the Village crowd at the time. Art Deco had never lived life to the max. Not even in school. He was never popular. He was always terribly introverted, with tons of complexes. The problem, as Arthur Deco Junior saw it, was Arthur Deco Senior, his father. Always pressuring him to do better; to be a better student than he was, to be a better athlete than he was, and eventually to be a better Chairman of the Board than Senior could've ever hoped to be. The pressure had a reverse effect. Junior didn't want to be any of those things.

Arthur Deco Junior was sent to Andover, the private school Arthur Deco Senior had attended; to Yale, the university Arthur Deco Senior had attended; and to Harvard Law School, the law school Arthur Deco Senior had attended. Junior was to become a lawyer and then Chairman of the Board of Deco Industries. It was all written in stone.

Arthur Deco Junior couldn't remember having a smidgen of fun during his entire education. That included grammar school. Having fun was not part of the Deco vocabulary. All the Deco family ever did was work. Not me, Junior swore to himself—he was going to have fun before being incarcerated for the rest of his natural life behind the walls of Deco Industries' home office in Bowling Green, Kentucky.

The first thing Arthur Deco Junior did was quit the law firm that employed him. Then young Deco went off to do some serious hell-raising. One example of Junior's idea of fun was hanging out with his two friends, Basil Sweeney and Ray Barno, two bozos of subnormal intelligence. The threesome generally trolled the Village whacked on high voltage hash one of them had scored. Why did Junior hang out with garbage? Simply because Barno and Sweeney let Art tag along. No one else would. Arthur Deco Junior was a dork.

Art's friends, Barno and Sweeney, were always broke. They either scrounged dinners from Salvation Army cafeterias or washed dishes in the kitchens of scuzzy little restaurants for meals. The two usually slept in shelters for the homeless.

Junior didn't eat in Salvation Army cafeterias or sleep in homeless shelters. When he was uptown and not slumming with his Neanderthal friends, wealthy Art Deco chose to eat in expensive East Side restaurants and sleep in his impressive apartment in a building on the corner of Eighty-third and Park Avenue, about as prestigious an address as you could find in Manhattan.

Art's apartment was a six-thousand-square-foot duplex, decorated with expensive furniture, paintings, and sculpture. It was here Art Deco brought New York's flotsam and jetsam, bums like Barno and Sweeney, other assorted ne'er-do-wells, scuzzy bimbos, and of course his buddies from the Sanitation Department.

The flotsam were impressed.

Junior's father, Arthur Deco Senior, had no idea what his son was up to and the life he was leading. God knows the size of the fit he would have had if he found out.

Senior's father, a hugely successful farmer named Ballard Deco, had been known as the Tobacco King of the South. Son Arthur returned from Korea, borrowed money from Ballard, and founded a small hardware store in the family's hometown of Bowling Green, Kentucky. The hardware store, driven by the son's ambition and ingenuity, evolved into Deco Industries: a conglomerate that included Deco Petroleum, Deco Pharmaceuticals, Deco Home-Owners Insurance Corporation of America, several radio and television stations, two newspapers, Deco Computer, Inc. (the backbone of the conglomerate), and the original hardware store.

Deco Industries employed nineteen thousand employees

worldwide, with plants and offices in Bowling Green, Houston, Chicago, New York, London, Hamburg, Rome, and Hong Kong. Father Ballard was Chairman of the Board, and son Arthur was Chief Executive Officer of the empire. Both Old Man Ballard and his son Arthur were rich and testy sons-of-bitches.

Upon his father's death, Arthur Deco assumed the title Senior.

Arthur Deco Senior married beautiful Margaret Hollingford when the two attended Western Kentucky University thirty-four years ago. The couple produced son Arthur (now age twenty-eight), the oldest of the Deco children, called Junior and heir to the throne; two married daughters, Harriet Deco Strange (twenty-six), called Hattie, Elizabeth Deco Brown (twenty-four), called Lizzie; and one unmarried daughter, Seena Deco (twenty-two). Arthur Deco Senior's family were Methodist and Republican.

Arthur Deco Senior and his daughter Mrs. Hattie Deco Strange were also extremely anti-Semitic, racist, and major homophobes.

It was a Saturday in late October when Arthur Deco Senior decided to have his son flown to his favorite mountain in Myles Standish State Park in Massachusetts, to see how the boy was getting on.

2

Senior had spotted the flat-topped mountain while flying as low as he could in his twin-engine Cessna Mustang. He had been on one of his solo trips from their home in Bowling Green, Kentucky, to the family compound in Camden, Maine. It was during these solo trips that Senior liked to "explore" the countryside just above the tree line. The flat-topped mountain was almost in the center of the Myles Standish State Forest. The good thing about the mountaintop was that two helicopters could land comfortably on its crown.

On this particular Saturday, Senior piloted his Bell 429 helicopter from Bowling Green to Massachusetts, with several stops along the way for fuel. The founder of Deco Industries owned two Bell helicopters. He kept one in New York, the one he sent to pick up his son. Junior was waiting at the helicopter pad on Thirty-fourth Street adjacent to the East River Drive in Manhattan. He was flown from there to the mountain.

Art Deco was sick and tired of thinking about seeing his father. It always meant trouble, sometimes severe trouble. The unseasonably cold, cloudy October weather only added to Junior's unhappiness and discomfort. Meeting his father usually augured a lecture, an argument, or both.

Junior was the first to arrive on the mountaintop. His father landed next. Arthur Deco Senior climbed out of his helicopter wearing his grandfather's hand-me-down World War I leather flying helmet that snapped on under his chin, a yellow scarf, and his Navy Air Force leather jacket with all his old squadron emblems sewn on it. Ballard Deco's father had used the leather flying helmet in World War I. Ballard had used it in World War II. His son, Arthur, had worn the flying helmet in Korea.

Arthur Deco Senior was furious when he saw his son. "My God, Junior, your hair looks like a girl's."

"Thank you, Father."

"I want you to cut it."

"It's the style, Father."

"It may be the style in Jew York, but I can tell you this. It is definitely *not* the style in Bowling Green, Kentucky."

The two men glared at each other. Both could hear the October wind blowing through the trees. Gray-black clouds skittered across the sky. The air was heavy with rain. Junior was freezing. He was only wearing a leather jacket and a black T-shirt that said UP YOURS in white letters on the front. The T-shirt was hidden by his buttoned-up jacket.

"From now on, Junior, when you come to meet me you dress accordingly. Understand?"

"Yes sir."

Junior wondered why he had never dressed "accordingly" when coming to see his father. Probably to get the automatic rise out of the old man he always got. He hoped one day the shock of seeing him not dressed accordingly would kill him. Cause the old goat to have a fatal heart attack, or a stroke, or something. Nothing would please Junior more than surprising his father in such a way as to cause his death. He daydreamed someone would telephone him someday to tell him his father had dropped dead on the street in Bowling Green. Fat chance. The old man was healthy as a horse. Junior was convinced Senior would outlive him by twenty years.

Tough as nails, was how most people described Arthur Deco Senior. And he was, thought Art. The mean bastard will die in bed over a hundred years old. No pain, no strain; just one minute his eyes are open, and the next they're shut. His family will be standing around his bed kissing his ass, or trying to, until the bitter end.

Art wouldn't be at his father's funeral. Seena would go grudgingly. His mother and sisters, mean Hattie and wishy-washy Elizabeth and their boot-licking husbands, would be standing around Senior's bed, along with the family's kowtowing butler, Donald. They all would be hoping for handouts. Hattie wishing her father would say, *Hattie, I want you to run the company.* Lizzie hoping he'd say, *Elizabeth, dear, I'm very proud of you. And always have been.* And Donald, the suck-up butler, praying the old bastard would say, *And Donald, I bequeath you one million dollars.* Fat chance of any of that happening.

"Do something about your goddamned hair, you hear?" barked Arthur Deco Senior, snapping Junior out of his daydream. "I want your hair looking normal, not like some kind of fairy, next time I see you."

"Yes sir."

"*Are* you a fairy, son? Don't lie to me."

"No, Father, I am *not* a fairy."

"What are you, then, with your damned long hair, and little diamond earring in the lobe of your ear, and all those . . . those . . . trinkets around your neck?"

"I'm me, Father."

"And what the hell kind of answer is that? 'I'm me.'"

"What do you *want* me to say, Father?"

"You're not ashamed of walking around the law firm with that pansy hairdo?"

"No, I'm not."

"And those clothes. Even though it's a weekend, how can a decent, churchgoing, American Christian wear clothes like that? Tell me, Junior, why . . . why do you wear such . . . such . . ."

"Clothing?" offered Junior.

"Yes." Senior sounded relieved. He was referring to Junior's black leather jacket with all the silver studs, and the thin, tight-fitting black leather pants that outlined his son's ass and balls.

"You wear watermelon slacks and sherbert-colored sweaters," said Junior, "and nobody yells at you. If that outfit doesn't look gay, I don't know what does."

"Be careful how you talk to me, son," said Senior, smiling an evil smile. As if a snake had tried to grin.

"Yes sir."

"While we're up here," said Art's father, "tell me this. Are you dating a Jew?"

"No."

"Are you dating a colored?"

"No."

"So what is it? You're guilty about something, so get it the hell off your chest. "

"I quit my job," confessed Junior. "I'm not working at Schatzberg, Downey, and Pels anymore."

"*You did what?* You quit working for— Do you know how many strings I pulled to get you that job? How hard I came down on that firm? I had to work like a dog to get you into Schatzberg, Downey, and Pels."

"I *know* how hard you pressured them to take me," said Junior. "Everyone in the law firm reminded me of that every single day. *That's* part of why I quit the damn job."

"What's the other part? Too many Jews in the law firm. *That* I could understand. If you had told me tha—"

"I don't want to be a lawyer, Father. I don't want to work in a law firm, because all that means is I'll be a lawyer for Deco Industries sooner or later."

"What's so bad about that? And it would only be for a short time. You'll be chairman of the board when I retire."

"Oh, come off it, Father, you're not going to retire. Not in *my* lifetime. Besides, I don't *want* to be Chairman of the Board of Deco Industries. That's no fun. I want to do something better with my life."

"Deco Industries isn't good enough for you? The business I built with my two hands, slaved over, worked in good times and bad, none of that's good enough for my only son? Well, *that's* interesting. So what is the 'something better' you want to be?"

"I want to be a veterinarian."

"A *what*? A veterinarian? You want to spend your life sticking your hand up a mare's doohickey feeling around for her foal?"

"Yes sir. That's what I want to do."

"Well, you can't be a veterinarian. It would be a disgrace if you didn't carry on the Deco name in the family business; the business I spent my entire working life building is *not* the business I'm going to give to a total stranger."

"Let Hattie run Deco Industries. She's always wanted to do that."

"I'm going to hand Deco Industries over to my *son,* and that's final."

3

There was something Junior didn't tell his father that windy afternoon on the mountaintop. Art didn't mention anything about the girl he intended to marry. Not yet. Art wanted to surprise Senior. But first he wanted to make sure he had her father's permission to marry. Art said nothing on the mountain because he didn't want to jinx getting the judge's approval.

The young lady Art Deco wanted to marry was Carrie Vandeveer.

They'd met on a blind date. Carrie was the youngest of four beautiful sisters in a prominent South Carolina family. Carrie Vandeveer was a friend of Art's sister Seena. The two girls went to the Mannerly Methodist Girls School, an exclusive—and expensive—girls' prep school outside of Columbia, South Carolina. Carrie was in her first year when Seena was in her last.

Seena Deco, who happened to be Junior's favorite sister, had arranged the blind date.

Carrie Vandeveer was nineteen years old and about to start her studies at Columbia University in Manhattan. She was going to be a doctor. Carrie visited New York on weekends looking for an apartment. She came on Friday afternoon and went home on Sunday.

When in Manhattan, Miss Vandeveer stayed at the Plaza Hotel. After Art's sister Seena had made the arrangements, Art Deco Junior had telephoned the Plaza and arranged to meet Carrie at seven-thirty that evening on what turned out to be a beautiful and unseasonably warm Friday night in November.

Miss Vandeveer seemed happy to hear that Mr. Deco was in the lobby and told him to come to her room immediately. When he arrived at Room 710 and finally saw Carrie Vandeveer in person, and heard her familiar thick Southern accent, Art Deco was transformed into a hapless bowl of Jell-O.

Carrie Vandeveer was five-foot-two with big blue eyes and strawberry blond hair. Her haircut made her hair curve around her head. Junior thought it was the cutest haircut he had ever seen in his entire life. Carrie Vandeveer instantly became the love of Art Deco's life. His sister Seena was thrilled.

"I am so happy to meet you, Arthur," said Carrie Vandeveer, standing in the open doorway of her room.

"Please call me Art."

"Fine. I'll call you just plain Art," said Carrie. "You see, Arthur, I've been so excited about meeting you it's taken me forever to get ready. How do I look, Arthur? Could you please zip me up?" Carrie turned her back and Art Deco zipped up her dress.

Art hated to be called Arthur. Everyone called his father Arthur. But when Carrie Vandeveer called Art Arthur, it sounded wonderful.

During dinner at Lusardi's on Second Avenue, Art had an idea.

"Would you mind coming to my apartment?" he asked. "I promise you on my word of honor, on my mother's life, and I love my mother, that I won't do anything bad. I mean, ungentlemanly. It's just such a nice clear night and the view of the city from my terrace, especially the George Washington Bridge, is beautiful. What do you think?"

Art talked very fast. He was almost out of breath when he finished.

Carrie Vandeveer laughed and said, "But Arthur, what if we *do* do something bad? Do you think your mother will be in danger?"

Junior was confused until Carrie said, "I'm teasing you. Let's go."

The pair stood on Art's terrace and looked at the George Washington Bridge off in the distance.

Carrie said, "It really is beautiful, Arthur."

"It is, isn't it?"

And then Carrie Vandeveer put her arms around Art Deco's neck and kissed him on his lips. For a long time.

Art pulled the young girl off the terrace and into his bedroom, where they made love for three days and nights, with breaks for meals, naps, and sleep. Once a day they'd go to the Plaza Hotel to grab a change of clothes for Carrie and gather up any messages from home she might have had.

Art Deco couldn't remember ever being so happy.

Carrie Vandeveer and Art Deco never missed a weekend. They seldom went out with friends. They ordered in most of the time and rarely left Art's bed from Friday night until Sunday afternoon, except to look for an apartment for Carrie. After a month Art Deco proposed marriage to Carrie Vandeveer.

"Unfortunately," she said, "you'll have to speak to Daddy."

"Unfortunately?"

"Yes," said Carrie. "I've been told Daddy's one tough cookie."

4

The New York Athletic Club was where Junior invited Judge Taylor Vandeveer to lunch to ask permission to marry the judge's youngest daughter. The father of the four pretty Vandeveer daughters was one of the justices of the United States District Court for the Eastern District of South Carolina.

Judge Vandeveer had been a former All-American lineman for the University of South Carolina's football team, a former Rhodes Scholar, and a Special Forces Green Beret. Judge Vandeveer was a highly decorated Army major who returned from the Vietnam War with a permanent limp. He was often mentioned for the South Carolina Senate seat, and lately was a possibility for the United States Supreme Court. He was a Republican, a conservative, a constitutional constructionist, severe at times, but reported to be a fair man.

Judge Vandeveer entered the main lobby of the NYAC, his cane firmly planted on the marble floor, his gaze covering the huge lobby like a searchlight. Not knowing what an Arthur Deco Junior looked like, the searchlight continued to swivel back and forth. Junior approached and introduced himself. The judge said nothing. Just smiled. Smiling was something the judge rarely did. It looked it.

Art led Judge Vandeveer to the elevators, then to the dining room, then to the table that was reserved in his name. Junior cleared his throat and said, "Thank you for coming. I appreciate your taking the time from your busy schedule to have lunch with me."

The judge didn't reply.

That bothered Junior and made him stumble over his next sentence. "I . . . uh . . . I . . . I want . . . I would like to—"

"I presume you want to talk about marrying my daughter Carrie. Is that correct?"

"Yes sir."

"How old are you?"

"Twenty-eight."

"Carrie just turned nineteen."

"Yes sir. I know, sir."

"She's very young."

"Yes sir. She is, sir."

There was a pause in the conversation while the two told the waiter what they wanted to eat. Art Deco didn't like either the tenor of the short conversation so far or the judge's tone of voice. He quickly concluded Judge Vandeveer would not give him permission to marry his daughter Carrie and immediately lost his appetite. But he ordered anyway.

When the waiter had gone, Judge Vandeveer continued. "What do you do, Deco?"

"Right now? I'm looking for a—"

"What have you done before now?"

"I graduated Harvard Law School."

"Then what?"

"I took a position with a law firm."

"Schatzberg, Downey, and Pels," said the judge.

"That's right, sir."

"But you left the firm, did you not?"

"Yes sir, I did."

"What do you intend to do with yourself now?"

"I'm not sure, sir."

"Not a good enough answer. What makes you think you can support my daughter, unemployed as you are and without any definite plans for the future?"

"I have a substantial trust fund."

"A trust fund that is at the whim of your father. Is that correct?"

"Yes sir. How do you know, sir?"

"I have my sources. Actually, Deco, your trust funds and your future are of little concern to me. What is of *great* concern to me is my daughter's education. Carrie is very young, Deco. I want her to complete her medical education. She will soon be starting her freshman year at Columbia University. I would have preferred if my daughter had matriculated at my alma mater, the University of South Carolina, where I went to school, but my daughter has a mind of her own."

Junior thought of how Carrie persisted in calling him Arthur, not Art.

"I am not entirely unhappy that Carrie has chosen Columbia," said the judge. "They do have an excellent medical school, and many excellent hospitals to choose from here in the city. In any case, I will see to it that Carrie finishes her four years at Columbia, her four years of medical school and one year of internship in general surgery, and then at least six years of neurosurgical training. If Carrie wants to specialize in, say, endoscopic removal of brain tumors, she may opt to take a few more years within the specialty."

"That's . . . that could be sixteen years from now . . . sir."

"Correct."

"But couldn't we be married while she's stud—"

"No. Out of the question. I do not want my daughter to be distracted by marital problems. I want her mind clear so that she can learn how to be a good surgeon."

Art Deco was devastated. He practically whispered, "Does *she* want—"

"It doesn't matter what *she* wants, Mr. Deco. It only matters what *I* want. I want my daughter to be a doctor. That is something she has always wanted to be, and I have always *wanted* her to be. I will not have Carrie distracted from her objective. I want her to finish her residency before she even thinks about a man in her life. I have a suggestion, Deco."

"Sir?"

"Forget about marrying my daughter. In fact, I will inform my daughter that you are off limits as far as she's concerned, until Carrie's finished her training."

Suddenly Art was angry. He gathered up his courage and said, "When your daughter is twenty-one, she can do whatever she wants, Judge Vandeveer."

"She most certainly can, Mr. Deco," said the judge, cold as ice, "but I very much doubt if she will defy her father."

Junior's short, happy life was over and lunch hadn't even been served.

TWO

THE
SUSPECT

I

Eddie Cantelone was a twenty-five-year-old lying, sleazy scuzzbag.

Eddie lived with his family in Flushing, New York, home of absolutely no one. Eddie's occupation was sponging off his family. His mother mistook her son's parasitic behavior for devotion, as most Italian parents do. His father never did.

When little Eddie Cantelone was ten years old, he made pick-ups and deliveries, collecting the numbers every day before he went to school for his bookie father, Salvatore Cantelone. He would return after school to pay off the winners. The winners would tousle Eddie's hair when he passed by. Losers never tousled. Eddie didn't want to make pick-ups and deliveries. That's because Eddie was lazy. His father made him do it.

When Eddie Cantelone was in his early twenties, his mother, Sophie, thought he was the spitting image of a young Dean Martin.

"A regular Prince of Flushing," Sophie Cantelone called her son.

Eddie Cantelone thought he was better-looking than Dean Martin. He considered himself "fuckin' handsome" as he so profoundly put it. The thing that made Eddie consider himself fuckin' handsome was that he could get any girl he wanted in Flushing, New York, which—unbeknownst to him—wasn't saying very much.

So, thought Eddie Cantelone, if I can get any babe in Flushing, why not parlay my good looks and dazzling personality into becoming rich and famous? And what better place to do that than Hollywood, California? So Eddie Cantelone decided to change his name to Eddie Cotton and migrate to the City of Angels.

When Eddie told his mother his plans to move to Hollywood, she cried her eyes out. Italian mothers cry a lot when their sons leave home. They also give their sons long, retarded dissertations on loyalty.

"Italian boys don't move away from their mothers," she wailed. "They stay with their mother so they can eat good and sit with their mother on the stoop and keep their mother company till she dies. Now I'm gonna have t'sit on the stoop alone and, worse, die alone."

"You'll have Papa," said an alert Eddie Cantelone.

"He'll be dead," said Eddie's mother, not missing a beat. "Italian boys sit with their mothers at least while their mothers are livin'. I never figured you sayin' somethin' like this, Eddie, not a good son like you. Listen t'me. I'm not gonna be around forever."

And then Eddie's mother sobbed as if she had been just diagnosed with pancreatic cancer.

Eddie cried right along with his mother. They both were sitting outside on their stoop. Neighborhood passersby thought nothing of the weeping Cantelones. Italians cry a lot.

Eddie rented a room in a tacky boardinghouse in Santa Monica. He took a job waiting tables in a health food restaurant on Montana Avenue called Health Heaven. As soon as he could afford it, he joined a gym and put a skimpy down payment on a beat-up second-hand red Saturn with a busted muffler. The car sounded like all hell breaking loose, but at least Eddie Cotton had transportation.

Whenever Eddie Cotton wasn't working at Health Heaven, he

was either at the gym building up his body or at the beach tanning himself. The tan he acquired helped him look even more handsome than he already was (he thought). His dark brown skin, dark brown Italian eyes, and jet-black Italian hair were a lethal mixture to the opposite sex (he thought). Plus there were Eddie's other features: his killing smile and muscular body. And don't forget he was a good dresser and clothes suited him (he thought).

But his love life, as Eddie put it, fuckin' sucked.

Ann Arbor would change all that.

2

Ann Arbor was young(ish), blond, and beautiful.

She was hot and she knew it. Unfortunately for Eddie, Ann Arbor was married. Fortunately for Eddie, Ann Arbor didn't let marriage stand in her way of a *schtup* or two, or three, or eighteen.

Ann Arbor was like most of the rich, bored, good-looking married women in Hollywood, Beverly Hills, Brentwood, Pacific Palisades, Santa Monica, Sherman Oaks, Encino, Santa Barbara, and Palm Springs. She fooled around.

Ann's husband Mel was rich as Croesus. He was the owner of a chain of trendy unisex clothing stores called PottsTown. While Mel ran PottsTown, Ann Arbor spent her time as a high-powered Hollywood agent. She represented stars and would-be stars.

Ann Arbor wasn't always Ann Arbor, nor was she always a high-powered talent agent. Her name used to be Rochelle Levy and she used to live in the Strawberry Mansion neighborhood of Philadelphia. When Ann was a teenager, she was the spitting image of Grace Kelly. So her mother changed her daughter's name and entered her into every beauty contest she could find. Ann Arbor became Miss Goldenberg's Peanut Chew of 1980 (when she was fourteen years old), Miss TastyKake (when she was sixteen), and Miss Altoona (when she was seventeen). Miss Altoona led to her becoming Miss Pennsylvania, which won her a trip to Atlantic City and the Miss America Beauty Pageant in 1982.

Ann Arbor, aka Rochelle Levy, came in third in the bathing suit competition and twelfth in the talent competition. She finished eighth overall. The recently divorced Mel Potts saw Ann Arbor on television doing her final walk up and down the runway. He had his secretary telephone Ann and invite her to come to Los Angeles.

Ann Arbor went.

Three days after she arrived, Mel and Ann were married in Las Vegas, Nevada. Mel Potts was a very rich man. Mel Potts and Ann Arbor had a deal. Mel liked having Ann on his arm and Ann liked spending Mel's money, which was typical of marriages in Hooray for Hollywood.

Mel Potts was always Mel Potts. He was five feet four inches tall, dark and Semitic-looking, with a long nose and big ears. Potts had married three times before Ann came along, and had three short, spoiled, dreadful-looking daughters to prove it, annoying souvenirs of each marriage. Faith, Hope, and Charity Potts were their names.

It was lust at first sight when Eddie Cotton's eyes met Ann Arbor's. The historic event took place in the weight room of the Santa Monica Health & Fitness Club. Incredible feelings started to zig and zag around Eddie's body like a dozen pinballs bouncing off his intestines, liver, gallbladder, and pancreas. Birds tweeting, heart thumping, loss of appetite; all new emotions for Eddie Cotton. He had never been in lust before.

Ann Arbor was always in lust. She liked the fact that a new swinging dick was in town, one she hadn't slept with . . . yet. The only male attribute that really mattered to Ann Arbor was the length of a dude's wiener schnitzel.

Ann Arbor had a button nose, brilliant blue eyes, scrumptious lips, a knockout face, flawless pink skin, "a great rack" (Eddie's words), a fabulous figure, and legs that wouldn't quit. She had thick yellow-white hair that fell to her shoulders. The way Ann's hair looked after she made love turned the Prince of Flushing on, big-time. Very few features of Ann Arbor's didn't turn the Prince of Flushing on. The fact that she had slept around didn't bother Eddie. It would have bothered Eddie's mother, though. She would have called Ann Arbor a *piccola puttana*.

(*Piccola puttana* means little whore.)

Ann Arbor was quite similar to a well-endowed female Mesothelae spider whose bite paralyzed her prey, then liquefied it. The spider drank the liquid and immediately started looking for more prey. That was Ann's MO. Her only problem: She was running out of prey. Eddie Cotton had no idea who he was messing with, nor how infinitely short his reign would be.

3

The carnal activities of Eddie Cotton and Ann Arbor pinnacled during the last two months of that year. Eddie's career was another story. It wasn't going anywhere.

That didn't stop Eddie from constantly telephoning his parents and all his relatives and friends in Flushing, telling them how successful he was becoming as an actor. He lied when he told everyone how he was up for a major television series starting next year, and—this was a secret—how he was going to be cast for a big-time movie.

"But I don't wanna talk about it," he told everyone at home. "I'm afraid I'm gonna jinx it. I just wanna say they're talkin' about me like I'm gonna be the next Al Pacino, but rougher and better-lookin'. Know what I mean? A rough tough Italian stud is how I'm bein' cast. And as far as my love life is concerned, I'm thinkin' about marryin' a beautiful big-time agent from out here."

Eddie Cotton figured Ann Arbor would leave Mel Potts for him in a heartbeat. Eddie began mulling over how Mrs. Ann Cotton would sound. He concluded it sounded great.

And then it happened.

4

"Whattaya mean, you don't want to see me anymore? Whattaya mean, I'm banished?" yelled Eddie Cotton, seeing little red flashes like miniature firecrackers exploding in front of his eyes. "Come on, Annie, whattaya fuckin' mean?"

"You understand English, I presume," replied Ann Arbor without emotion, cold as an icicle. "What I mean is, as I told you on the telephone last night, I do *not* want to see you anymore, which—for your information—*includes my office*. The next time you come here I'll have security throw you the hell out."

"You're talkin' crazy, Annie. We're a pair born in heaven. You're my soul mate."

"I am nothing of the kind, you imbecile. What a weird conception. You were a good lay and nothing more, Eddie, and now I have a better lay. So *hasta la* fuckin' *vista*, as *you* would say."

"I don't believe you, Annie. I don't fuckin' believe you."

"One last thing," she said. "I *hate* to be called Annie."

Though Ann Arbor thought the ultimatum she laid down in her office would do the trick, it didn't. It wasn't easy to get rid of lovesick Eddie Cotton. Ann had to have Eddie thrown out of her office building three more times. Each occasion embarrassed her to the bone.

When Eddie no longer bothered Ann at her office, she noticed him lurking on street corners when she left the building. There was nothing more creepy-crawly than looking at her automobile's rearview mirror in heavy traffic and seeing Eddie Cotton's face leering back at her a car length behind. Or seeing his car trailing behind her Bentley on the winding roads at night near her home. Several times when she pulled her Bentley into her garage and walked briskly to her front door, Eddie was parked across the street watching her.

And then there was the infamous early evening in December when Ann walked outside to inspect the hydrangeas the gardner had just planted. That's when Eddie Cotton's old beat-up red Saturn jumped the curb onto the pavement, then onto the neighbor's lawn, and started heading directly for Ann Arbor. She couldn't do anything but turn and run for her life. As she ran she could hear the bump-de-bump-de-bump of the red Saturn's tires going over her neighbor's lawn and driveway, then *her* lawn and driveway.

Ann Arbor ran to the porte cochere of the home next door. The driveway led to the grounds behind her neighbor's mansion and to a swimming pool. Ann Arbor jumped into the pool. It was only then that she rid herself of the feeling of impending doom.

The home owner, a woman, came running out of her house screaming, "There's an automobile on my front lawn. There's an automobile on my front lawn."

"Please call the police, Mrs. Donahue," said Ann Arbor calmly, "and tell them that." Ann Arbor was standing fully clothed and freezing in the middle of the woman's pool. (The bitch hadn't turned on the pool heater.)

By the time the police came, Eddie Cotton and his Saturn from hell were gone.

THREE

The Victim Meets the Suspect

I

Eddie Cotton sat quietly in the back seat of a taxicab in front of the arrivals area at Kennedy International Airport. He had just returned to Manhattan from Los Angeles, his tail between his legs. First, he had been dumped by Ann Arbor, his "soul mate" and the love of his life. Second, he wasn't a movie star. Third, he didn't even have a small part in a cable television series. And fourth, he didn't have any money.

"I'm a friggin' failure, is what I am," he said to himself.

"What did you say?" said the cabdriver. "You just say something?"

"No," said Eddie Cotton.

"So where to, buddy?" said the cabbie for the third time. "We can't sit here all day, you know."

"Fuck if I know where to."

"How 'bout I take you to the McBurney YMCA on West Fourteenth Street?" said the cabdriver. "They have cheap rooms there and it's a nice place."

So that's where they went.

"This whole goddamn place smells of chlorine," said Eddie to the admissions guy.

"Yep," he answered. "It sure does. But you get used to it."

The repulsive odor was everywhere: in his room, in his closet, even on his sheets and pillows. The smell came from the swimming pool in the Y's basement. In time, like the man said, Eddie got used to it.

Every day Eddie Cotton checked the want ads in the newspapers. He found nothing that interested him. Actually, he really didn't want to work. But he didn't like wandering the streets of New York's West Side, either. It was January. He froze outside and was claustrophobic inside.

He lost his appetite, and didn't sleep much at night. He wrestled with the idea of going home. He could be eating his mother's great cooking and sleeping in his cozy old bed. But after all the boasting he'd done, that was impossible. He'd be ridiculed until the day he died.

2

Eddie Cotton was sitting at the bar of a restaurant on the corner of Tenth Street and Eighth Avenue, nursing a lukewarm cup of coffee. It was the lunch hour of a particularly raw January afternoon.

The restaurant's chef was known for his omelets, something the restaurant was moderately famous for, at least in the neighborhood. A description of the omelet-of-the-day was written in red chalk on a blackboard nailed to a wall where everyone in the restaurant could see it. The featured omelet that day was one with prosciutto, spinach, and tomato. Eddie Cotton, sitting at the far end of the bar, would have loved the day's featured omelet. He really liked prosciutto. But he couldn't afford it. He was down to his last dollar. The crumpled bill was in his pants pocket.

Eddie didn't have a choice. He was forced to sit in that miserable restaurant as long as he could, staring at his, by now, cold cup of coffee. It was a hell of a lot better than wandering the streets freezing to death, or sitting in a room that stank to high heaven from chlorine.

Just when you think you have life by the balls, mused Eddie, somethin' bad always happens. It never works the other way around, does it? I mean, when you're down on your luck, nothin' good ever happens, does it? Like what the hell am I gonna do for money? It seemed to be the only question on his mind. Night and day. Asleep or awake. Always thinking, What am I gonna do for money? What am I gonna do for money? Thing was, he never thought of a good answer.

"Cold as a well-digger's asshole at twenty fathoms," said a bedraggled old noonday drunk sitting on Eddie Cotton's left. The drunk flicked some spittle on Eddie's coat sleeve when he spoke. "All I have to my name is this damn sweater," said the old drunk to Eddie. The bum pointed to a hole in his sweater. "At least it's a holy sweater." The bum produced a phlegmy cackle.

Being in the company of a drunken old bum depressed Eddie. "Shut the fuck up an' don't talk to me anymore, you hear?" he growled to the old drunk, and went back to his dark thoughts.

In some respects it's lucky I got outta Dodge when I did, he decided. That Jew bastard Potts would have had my ass arrested. And now all I have to show for my time in La La Land is a maxed-out credit card and a dollar in my pants pocket.

"*You* shut the fuck up," lisped a toothless old hag with a rat's nest for hair, and no teeth. She was sitting on the far side of the old bum. She was either the drunk's girlfriend or his wife. She leaned forward in front of the old bum so she could see Eddie Cotton and he could see her.

Before Eddie Cotton could yell back at the toothless hag, the bartender said, "You gonna sit there all day nursing that one cup a coffee?"

The bartender was a big muscular guy wearing a red bandanna around his head and a purple sweatshirt that said METS in orange on it. Though it was the middle of winter, the bartender's sweatshirt was cut off at the shoulders. The bartender wanted to show off the massive tattoos on his arms.

"Any law against nursin' a cup a coffee, Tattoo Man?"

"Yeah, my law. It's lunchtime and I get customers who wanna spend money."

"You know what you can do with your goddamned law," said Eddie Cotton.

"Here's your check. Go pay it and get the hell outta here."

"Yeah, get the hell outta here," screamed the toothless old hag, this time looking at Cotton from behind the old drunk.

"Up yours," said Eddie. "Go suck off your buddy and shut the fuck up, why don'tcha?"

Eddie Cotton got off the stool, looked at his check and whirled around to face the bartender. *"A dollar sixty-seven for a friggin' cup of coffee?"* he yelled.

"Just pay the check, pal, and scram," snarled the bartender.

"You gotta lot of fuckin' nerve, chargin' that much money for a lousy cup a coffee," said Eddie Cotton. "And I ain't your pal, so don't fuckin' call me that."

"Hey, buddy, watch your mouth," said the bartender.

"I'm not your fuckin' buddy either," yelled Eddie, pushing his finger practically into the bartender's face.

The bartender started lifting up the wooden panel so he could get out from behind the bar. Eddie quickly turned and walked toward the cash register.

"You gotta check?" asked the cashier.

"Yeah, I gotta check. What happened to the fifty-cent cup of coffee?" Eddie asked.

"Dunno," said the man standing behind the register. The cashier wore a turban on his head. He was Indian or something.

"Does this fuckin' city have any Americans in it anymore?" Eddie Cotton asked the man behind the cash register. He laid the dollar bill and the check down next to the cash register and turned to leave.

"Hey, you owe me sixty-seven cents," said the cashier. "Do you have sixty-seven cents?"

"No, I don't," said Eddie Cotton.

"I need sixty-seven cents," insisted the clerk.

"Hey, raghead, I only have a goddamn dollar," snapped quick-to-anger Eddie Cotton, seething, leaning across the counter so he could be in the clerk's face, seeing those little red firecrackers going off in front of his eyes. "You gonna call the cops for sixty-seven cents, raghead?"

Everyone in the restaurant was looking at Eddie Cotton, including the bartender at the far end of the room, who was lifting his wooden panel again, to come to the defense of the cashier.

"You owe me sixty-seven cents," said the stubborn cashier, unafraid.

"Maybe if you were nicer to the cashier he would let you bring the sixty-seven cents back tomorrow," said a voice behind Eddie's back.

Eddie whirled around again, just about at the end of his tether, the red firecrackers going off behind his eyes. It looked like the Fourth of July in his head. Eddie blinked and looked again. What he saw was a pleasant-looking young man holding up a five-dollar bill.

"I've got his check," said Arthur Deco Junior.

3

Art Deco paid Eddie Cotton's check. The two walked out onto busy Eighth Avenue. It was freezing. There was a strong wind that day. It blew newspapers and trash up against their legs. Everyone walking looked cold. They kept their hands in their pockets and their chins pressed down against their coat fronts. Some had their scarves wrapped around their mouths and ears.

Art Deco wore a blue cashmere overcoat, a maroon scarf, black leather gloves, and earmuffs. Eddie wore an old wool jacket and a Yankees baseball hat. He kept his hands in his pockets. He didn't have any gloves. The two young men started walking north.

"Name's Eddie Cotton."

"Art Deco."

"Thanks for jumpin' in and savin' me from making an even bigger fool of myself," said Eddie Cotton, trying his best to suck up to the stranger. Eddie figured, by the look of his clothes, this Deco guy was a rich son-of-a-bitch. "Don't know what got into me. Lately I seem to have a short fuse. I've always had a short fuse, but lately it seems shorter than ever. Don't know why."

"Obviously I don't know you, but maybe you're discouraged," suggested Art Deco. "I've got a short temper too when I'm discouraged."

"I wasn't known for a hell of a lot of patience on a good day, Art. Maybe it was the bumps I took out in Los Angeles."

"I had some bumps too," said Art Deco.

"Tell me about your bumps," said Eddie.

"Well, first of all," said Art, prone to confess to anyone, "I had to break up with my girlfriend."

"That sounds familiar," said the suck-up.

The two turned and walked east at Forty-ninth Street. At Park Avenue, they went north to Eighty-third and Park. It was a long walk and the two talked all the way. The time went by quickly. When they arrived at Art Deco's apartment building, Art had told Eddie Cotton his entire life's story, including the bad parts: the drugs, the idiots he ran with, his being fat, Judge Vandeveer, losing the girl of his dreams, and the dismal prospect of him having to go back to Bowling Green, Kentucky, to run the family business.

In the lobby of Art Deco's apartment building the two sat on a couch and continued talking. It was Eddie's turn. He told Art everything that had happened to him in California. Almost. Eddie mentioned being dumped by Ann Arbor, but omitted the part about his trying to run her down with his Saturn from hell.

He made up a wild story to explain his sudden departure from Los Angeles. Something about his boss at Health Heaven, a Mexican named Luis "Fat Louie" Navarro. He told Art Deco that Fat Louie ordered his gang to kill Eddie for messing with his girlfriend. Eddie said it was all a big mistake, said the girl came on to *him,* and because of her advances and Fat Louie's temper, Eddie feared for his life. He had to leave Los Angeles so quickly, he didn't have time to pack any of his things.

Eddie made up reasons why he couldn't go back to his family in Flushing. He explained that he didn't want to be a financial burden to his almost destitute parents. Eddie said, "To tell you the truth, I don't ever wanna go back to Flushing, if I can help it."

"And I don't want to ever go back to Bowling Green either," said Art Deco.

Both men got to know each other quickly and well. The two wallowed in each other's miseries, and commiserated with each other's broken hearts.

4

In February, one month from the day they met, Eddie Cotton moved into Art Deco's plush duplex on Park Avenue.

"This is just until you get settled," said Junior.

Eddie's bedroom was huge. The room had a large window facing Central Park. Another window faced north, with a view of upper Fifth Avenue. The bed, in Eddie's eyes, was as big as a basketball court. There were tons of pillows, the softest, fanciest sheets, and a thick comforter to keep Eddie warm.

Eddie Cotton's possessions filled half of one drawer of the large bureau. There was a couch with big stuffed pillows across it, a coffee table in front of the couch, and a comfortable armchair with a matching ottoman. Art Deco had a cook to make their meals and a housekeeper to clean up after them.

"I don't know what to say," were the first words out of Eddie's mouth, *after* he moved in.

"You're my friend," said Art Deco, "and I have more rooms than I need. I couldn't see you staying in that fleabag YMCA a moment longer. This is just until you get settled, you know, with an apartment of your own and a job. Hey, we're both still hung over and depressed from Christmas. Bleak, freezing February is not the time

47

of year to be alone. We've been pounded by the elements. We'll take this time to recoup and buck each other up."

Eddie felt the sharp scratch of disappointment when Art said, "This is just until you get settled." He'd said it twice.

The first night Eddie went to sleep in his temporary new digs, he lay in bed staring at the ceiling thinking about a lot of what-ifs. What if I had left the French Toast Restaurant a half hour earlier? What if I'd had enough money to pay the check? What if Art had gone somewhere else for lunch? What if . . .

. . . until he fell asleep.

5

The "just until you get settled" edict lasted for several years.

Art and Eddie became good friends. Art resurrected his original good manners, and resumed his soft-spoken, mannerly ways. He dieted and exercised, didn't do the heavy drinking he used to do, and he abstained totally from all drugs. Art rapidly lost the weight he'd gained and started looking good again, all of which he wrote off to Eddie Cotton's positive influence.

Eddie Cotton turned over a bunch of new leafs too. Now that he was in such high-class company, he wanted to try and better himself as fast as he could. He allowed Art Deco to teach him manners. He watched dropping his *g*'s, kept his voice down, and didn't discuss subjects he knew nothing about.

Neither one, however, had taken the time to find jobs.

Eddie Cotton began leaving a trail of lies to both Art Deco and his parents. He told his mother and father he had moved back to New York because of a better business opportunity. He said he was a big-shot agent now with the William Morris Talent Agency. He lied about how much money he was making. He lied about where he lived. He told his parents he had joined two other guys and shared the expenses of an apartment on ritzy Park Avenue. He gave them Art's address in case his parents wanted to write him. He lied about his nonexistent Porsche convertible. He told his parents he had driven the sports car across the country and was keeping it in a garage in Manhattan.

Eddie forbade his parents to drop by his apartment unexpectedly. He said it was the unanimous decision of all three roommates that no one would be allowed to come to the apartment without telephoning first. The rule prevented embarrassing situations.

"Telephone first," repeated Eddie, and gave his parents the number of the line Art had installed for his personal use.

Eddie told his mother and father he wanted them to come visit but he was off to Europe on a talent hunt and might be gone for a long time. He would try and see them before he left. He refused to give his parents a work phone number, claiming his boss at the talent agency frowned on personal phone calls. Eddie warned his parents that if they tried to find his number and telephoned, he could lose his job.

Sal and Sophie Cantelone were confused by their son's decrees, but obeyed them implicitly.

Before Eddie Cotton departed on his fictitious business trip to Europe, he went to visit his parents in Flushing. He drove a new Porsche convertible Art had rented him. He was immaculately dressed in a Brooks Brothers suit, tie, brown pigskin gloves, and topcoat Art had bought him. It was an extremely uncomfortable meeting for both Eddie and his parents. Eddie was having trouble keeping track of his lies. His parents thought him more a stranger than a son. The visit seemed to go on forever. Eddie was thrilled when he finally got to leave and go back to the city.

Sophie was distraught by her son's visit. She thought he looked and acted strangely. She said, "He even changed his name, Salvatore. All of a sudden he's Eddie Cotton. I miss my Eddie Cantelone."

Sal could have broken Eddie's forehead for making his mother so sad.

Art asked Eddie once or twice about the possibility of meeting Eddie's parents. Eddie sidestepped the request until Art stopped asking. Eddie Cotton wasn't permitted to see Art's family either. Art hadn't told his parents or his three sisters about his new roommate for fear his father would misunderstand the situation. Art wondered, now and then, if there was a situation to misunderstand. An unwritten rule developed between the two men: Families were verboten.

As far as Eddie Cotton was concerned, living with Art Deco was a dream come true. He had just one worry. He wondered if he would wake up one day and find that Art Deco had found someone else, maybe a girl he decided to marry. Then he would kick Eddie out of his apartment. Ann Arbor all over again. It was too scary to think about, so Eddie didn't.

The fact that neither Eddie nor Art ever dated girls was also somewhat odd. Eddie Cotton stopped thinking about that too.

Instead, Eddie Cotton continued to luxuriate in Art Deco's generosity. Art bought Eddie clothes, rented him sports cars, picked up lunch and dinner checks, even gave Eddie an allowance every week. The two didn't go out much, but when they did Art always paid for their theater or concert tickets.

A year had passed. And then one evening at dinner Art Deco said, "Eddie, I want you to come with me to Europe."

"No shit," said Eddie excitedly. "I ain't never never been to Europe."

"I *haven't* ever been to Europe," corrected Art Deco sternly.

They left for Paris, London, and Rome in June.

It was in Paris where the event that would change both their lives took place.

6

Their first night in Paris, Art led the way down a dark alley until they reached a small bistro called Chez Ami Louis.

Art told Eddie, "Chez Ami Louis has the best roast chicken in the entire world. And the best onion rings. And the best french fries. And . . . well . . . the best *everything*."

The two friends ate a delicious, simple salad covered with the lightest but tastiest dressing. The waiter brought out a huge slab of Art's favorite foie gras. Eddie had never tasted foie gras before. He loved it and helped himself to gobs of the paste.

"Hold it, Eddie," barked Art Deco. "They're not giving it away. You pay for every ounce of the stuff."

When the morels, in a light cream sauce, were placed on their table, Eddie asked if he could take as much as he wanted. Art assured him he could. Finally the waiter served them the restaurant's famous *poulet roti*, sizzling in a black roasting pan. The roast chicken's skin was stiff and crackly, resembling brown parchment paper. Its soft, delicious meat underneath was better than anything Eddie Cotton had ever tasted in his entire life. The two ate Chez Ami Louis's delectable *pommes frites* and fried onion rings, and drank two bottles of '96 Haut-Brion.

"Best dinner I've ever eaten," declared Eddie Cotton.

"I told you," said Art Deco.

After dinner, stuffed to the point of being uncomfortable, tipsy from the wine they'd drunk, and overwhelmed with friendship toward each other, the two wandered down the alleylike street, arms around each others' shoulders, until they came to the Boulevard Saint-Germain. Off the boulevard was the Pont de la Concorde bridge. The pair walked to the middle of the large bridge. Cars and taxis went whizzing by in both directions. There was a breeze that was absolutely balmy.

The two stopped in the middle of the bridge to watch a Bateau Mouche, with its festive strings of little white lights, float by on the Seine beneath them. The boat was filled with dining tourists seated at tables inside the floating restaurant or watching the city go by from the top deck. Small squares of yellow lights from apartments dotted the black night on both sides of the River Seine.

Standing on the Pont de la Concorde, Art Deco and Eddie Cotton followed the Bateau Mouche until it disappeared under them. It seemed like the perfect ending to a wonderful day and night in Paris. Eddie and Art looked at the river over the short cement wall, Art with his arm across Eddie's shoulders.

They stared at the river for a bit, then turned and kissed each other on the mouth, as the taxis and automobiles drove by.

7

It was a spontaneous, spur-of-the-moment decision seemingly on both their parts. The kiss lasted for a long time. When they pulled away from each other, Art Deco and Eddie Cotton wondered the same thoughts in tandem: Were we too drunk to know what we were doing? Did it matter if we were?

After a moment's pause, Eddie Cotton threw his arms in the air as if he were just declared the winner of the heavyweight boxing championship of the world, and yelled, *"I'm so relieved."*

"Me too," said Art Deco quietly, wondering if that was how he truly felt. "It feels as if the weight of the world has been lifted off my shoulders."

"Yeah," said Eddie Cotton.

"Yes," corrected Art Deco.

"Yes," said Eddie Cotton, still excited, still in awe of his emotions. "I feel the same way. For the first time in my life I can think straight. I had to become a *queer* to think *straight*." Eddie Cotton laughed at his play on words.

"I hate that word, Eddie."

"What word?"

"Queer. We're not *queer*, Eddie . . . are we?"

Eddie Cotton said quickly, "Not at all."

Art Deco put his arm around Eddie Cotton's shoulders and said, "I think we should celebrate this monumental night forever."

"At least for the next month," said Eddie.

And they did.

The pair never made it to London or Rome as planned. They were enjoying Paris too much. For several nights the two watched Paris go by as passengers on a Bateau Mouche. They stood on the bow of the boat in agreeable silence and held hands as they passed under the Pont de la Concorde.

During their second week they made love in their new and slightly scary world of homosexuality. The transition was easy and natural. Afterward, the two felt a whole lot better about themselves.

Art and Eddie spent their last two weeks in Paris making love and being tourists. They visited Notre Dame Cathedral. Eddie Cotton was a lapsed Catholic and Art Deco a Methodist. Cotton crossed himself inside the cathedral while Deco watched. Then Art crossed himself too, knelt, and said a prayer.

When they were outside, Eddie asked Art what he'd prayed for.

"Us."

"Me too."

On their last night in Paris, the two returned to the restaurant Chez Ami Louis, and ordered the same dinner they had before. After dinner the two decided to reenact their first night in Paris. The pair were tipsy as they walked toward the Boulevard Saint-Germain, arms around each other's shoulders as they did on their first night, stopping along the way to kiss each other.

Three skinny roughnecks ran past them. One of the toughs bumped his shoulder hard against Art's as he passed. Art and Eddie stopped walking and turned to face the three hoodlums, but the hoodlums kept running. And then one turned and yelled, *"Les pedes."*

Faggots.

8

After the new year Art Deco decided to look for a summerhouse on the beach in the Hamptons. The two didn't find anything they liked there, so they kept looking farther and farther away from the city. The real estate agent told Art about a rustic old "tear-down" in Montauk.

"It has possibilities," said the real estate lady.

Montauk was a four- to five-hour drive from Manhattan, depending on what time the two left the city and how bad the traffic was.

"Jesus, Art, we'll be drivin' all day."

"You're dropping your *g*'s, Eddie."

The ramshackle cottage had two front doors.

"How come?" Eddie asked the real estate lady.

"How come what?"

"How come two front doors?"

"This place used to be a tavern," she said. "One door was for men and one was for women."

Bullshit, thought Eddie Cotton. It may have been a tavern, but one door was for blacks and one for whites.

The dilapidated exterior of the house was painted an awful

reddish purple. It had ancient windows with church-spire window frames, and at one time, according to the dowdy real estate woman, there was a deck facing the ocean.

"The house used to have a deck," said the real estate lady. "Unfortunately, the deck collapsed during a strong winter storm and was washed out to sea. But there's room to build another one."

Strong winter storm my ass, thought Eddie Cotton. A drizzle knocked that deck away.

The two followed the real estate lady inside the house to look around.

"What do you think so far?" Art asked Eddie when the real estate lady stepped out of the room.

"I think the house is a disaster waiting to be washed out to sea," he answered. "You're going to buy it, aren't you, Art?"

"I think so. We can really fix it up and make it look cozy as hell."

9

Eddie Cotton and Art Deco were very happy living in their two New York residences; their apartment at Eighty-third and Park, and their beach house that their new architect Tim Duncan helped design and refurbish in Montauk. Both Eddie and Art liked Tim Duncan, who modeled in his spare time. Duncan had been recommended by a Deco family friend who lived in New York. Both Eddie and Art got along well with Tim.

Eddie Cotton's loudness and speech—mainly dropping his *g's*—embarrassed Art more and more. Eddie was constantly aware of this and made an effort to do better. He was quick to correct himself, and tried his best to remember not to talk so loudly.

Art began flying lessons at the East Hampton Airport. This pleased Art's father tremendously.

"I told Junior if he got his license, I'd buy him a plane," Arthur Deco Senior told his wife. "You know, Mother, the boy might be coming around. He dresses like a gentleman again. He's cut his hair. I think Junior's trying to impress me."

"Has he gotten a job yet?" asked Senior's wife.

When Art traveled to Kentucky to visit his family, he and his father would drive to the Bowling Green airport to see if there was a plane there similar to the one Senior wanted to buy Junior. A Cessna T182.

"It's a simple craft to fly," said Senior. "The plane has docile flight characteristics, holds four people, is reliable and economical. When will you get your license, son?"

"If I take a lesson every day, I'll have my license in March, depending on the weather," said Art Deco Junior.

Art's father beamed.

Eddie Cotton began taking lessons too. He became a good horseback rider and, to his amazement, an excellent painter. The painting came naturally. He didn't need lessons for that. Eddie specialized in watercolor beach scenes. Art dealers in the Hamptons considered Eddie's beach scenes extremely good. Art built a small studio on the Montauk property for Eddie.

"I have never been so happy," Art Deco told Eddie Cotton one evening as they sat in the living room of their New York apartment. "Are you as happy as I am, Eddie?"

"Almost."

"Almost? What do you mean, almost?"

"I don't feel secure, Art. I mean, I'm very happy living with you. As a matter of fact, I've never been this happy in my entire life, startin'—I mean starting with—our night in Paris, even before that. But I've *never* felt secure."

"Never."

"Never," said Eddie. "What would I do if you left me, Art? I'm not getting any younger, you know."

"That will never happen, Eddie," Art said angrily. "How many times do I have to tell you that?"

"Still, you could, you know."

"But I won't. Ever."

Eddie Cotton could tell he was pushing Art Deco. Art got a certain expression on his face when he was becoming annoyed. He had that expression then. But Eddie persevered.

"But what if you *do* find someone else?" said Eddie. "What security against my old age do I have then?"

Art Deco stood and walked out of the room.

The two didn't talk to each other for the rest of the evening. That night Art told Eddie he was going to sleep in the guest bedroom. Eddie shrugged his shoulders. They had separate breakfasts. But that afternoon Art joined Eddie for lunch.

"You're right, Eddie," he said

"About what?" asked Eddie looking up, as if he didn't know.

"About what we talked about last night. I spoke to Sidney Bricker this morning and explained the problem to him."

"Who's Sidney Bricker?"

"The family lawyer."

"The *family lawyer*," yelled Eddie, not the least bit concerned that he was shouting. "You went to the *family lawyer?* Why the fuck would you do somethin' like that, Art?"

"Why not?"

"Why not? Because the *family lawyer* will go directly to your goddamned father without stoppin' to take a whiz, and tell him. That's why."

"No, he won't. Sidney promised me our conversation would be confidential. Lawyer-client stuff. Anyway, Sidney suggested I put you in my will, if that's agreeable to you. When I die, whatever I have in my estate will go to you. This apartment, the Montauk house, whatever monies I'm left in my parents' wills, the Bentley, everything that's in my name will—"

"No way, José," said Eddie Cotton.

"*What?*" said Art, surprised.

"Art, do you think I was born yesterday or somethin'? Come on. Even I know wills can be changed. They're changed every day of the week. And you can change your will without me even knowin' it. Puttin' me in your will, this great idea of your family lawyer's, is a big crock of shit."

"Eddie—"

"I'm tellin' you, Art, wills don't mean a goddamn thing. So I'm in your will. So what? An' just like that, I'm outta your fuckin' will. Puttin' me in your will doesn't protect me from a fuckin' thing, Art. That's just a lot of flim-flam."

There was a big silence.

"You're dropping your *g*'s, Eddie."

"Yeah, an' I'm cursin' an' I'm raisin' my voice too. So what?"

Art Deco went silent, and stayed that way for a while. Eddie Cotton could tell he was either thinking or getting mad again.

"Okay," he said. "Forget about the will. I'll open a savings account and put money in it for you."

"How much money?"

"A million dollars."

"That's not enough."

"*Not enough?*" yelled Art Deco. Then, simmering down, he said, "How about five million dollars?"

"How about ten?" said Eddie. "You're rich, Art. You can afford ten. Besides, if you never leave me, the money stays in your pocket."

"For that amount of money, I'm going to have to talk to Sidney Bricker again."

"Then talk to Sidney Bricker," said Eddie Cotton, his heart beating wildly.

The next evening at dinner, a smiling Art Deco presented Eddie Cotton with a bank book.

"Mind if I check it?" he asked.

"Not at all."

Eddie opened the bankbook and went directly to the total. It read: *$10,000,000.*

"Satisfied?" asked Art.

"The problem's history."

Art asked one of their maids to bring a bottle of champagne from the fridge. When she did, Art popped the cork and the two men clinked champagne glasses to celebrate Eddie Cotton's security.

Eddie was too excited to see the bankbook had Art Deco's name on it too. And he wasn't wise enough to know the good and bad parts of a joint bank account.

10

In the months to come, Eddie Cotton and Art Deco were seen everywhere together. The two seemed to have come out of the closet.

Art wasn't nervous about it.

But Eddie was.

"I think we should stop doin' what we're doin', Art."

"I don't. I want everyone to know we're together. Don't you?"

"Well, no, to be honest with you," said Eddie, "I don't want *my* parents to know. And I wouldn't be too thrilled if *your* parents knew. You said you weren't gonna tell your father we were livin' together until *after* he bought you your plane."

"I'm *not* going to tell my father. You're dropping your g's, Eddie. You shouldn't talk when you're nervous."

"Jesus, Art, he sure as shit'll find out if we keep doin' what we're doin'."

"*Stop dropping your* g*'s, Eddie.*" Then, calming down, Art said, "Relax, for Christ's sake. So what if my father finds out? I don't care if he does. I'm tired of not being able to go anywhere, Eddie. I want to go to the theater and to sporting events. I'm sick and tired of staying home all the time."

"We don't stay home all the—"

"Shut up, Eddie."

The two continued going to movies, museums, plays, the opera, the symphony, the ballet, and Rangers, Knicks, Yankees, and Giants games. Art Deco was overdoing it. He acted as if he was purposely trying to create a problem with his father.

Eventually the inevitable happened. Word got back to Arthur Deco Senior in Bowling Green from his New York cronies. They told Senior his son had been seen in the company of the same man over and over again. Senior became suspicious, then angry, then enraged.

The situation called for a helicopter ride.

Junior was notified to meet his father at Teterboro Airport the following Saturday.

Eddie, not Art, was a nervous wreck.

"He knows. I know he knows," Eddie said.

"Of course he knows. So what?"

"Somethin' terrible's gonna happen, Art. I know it. I just *know* it."

"What can happen? He can't break us up. If he takes my trust away, I still have my grandparents' trust. So what can he do?"

"Your grandparents' trust isn't as big as your parents'. We'll have to cut back. But that won't be so bad, I suppose, as long as we're together."

"Right," said Art Deco. "It won't be so bad."

"On second thought, Art, your father won't just disinherit you. He'll do somethin' worse. Much worse. He'll make *me* leave, *that's* what he'll do. He'll pressure you into makin' me go away. Your father won't put up with his son livin' with another man. He'll find some way to make me go away." During the conversation, Eddie's voice seemed to rise and rise. "He'll . . . he'll . . . he'll make you come to work in Bowlin' Green and not take me. He'll threaten you with—"

"Calm the fuck down, Eddie."

"I'm upset," said Eddie Cotton softly.

Art had his new African-American chauffeur, Howard, drive him to Teterboro in Art's new Bentley. At Teterboro, Art met his father and they both transferred to Senior's helicopter. The old man piloted his New York–based helicopter to the mountaintop, going all the way with an angry expression on his face, and never saying a word to his son. Arthur Deco Senior landed the helicopter on the Massachusetts mountaintop in Myles Standish State Forest. He jumped out and ran to the edge of the clearing, as he always did. Junior followed.

When Art arrived by his father's side, Senior turned and shouted, red-faced, "Are you a faggot?"

"Yes, Father, I'm a faggot," Junior shouted back. "Though I prefer to be called gay."

FOUR

THE DECOS

I

When Senior returned to Bowling Green, he called a family meeting. Present were his wife, Margaret; his two married daughters, Mrs. Hattie Deco Strange and Mrs. Elizabeth Deco Brown; and the Decos' youngest daughter, Seena Deco.

"I have an announcement to make," said Arthur Deco Senior in his serious voice. "Junior is gay."

Daughter Hattie gasped. "How do you know?"

"I heard it first from friends who live in New York. And then I had a meeting with Junior yesterday afternoon and asked him face-to-face if he was gay. And he answered that he was.

"Good for him," said Seena.

"Good for *him*?" repeated Hattie Strange.

Seena Deco was a skinny thing. She was flat as a board front and back but had a pretty face, and a mop of red curly hair on top of it, a present from her mother. Seena Deco always wore black horn-rimmed glasses. And when Seena got mad, she got very, very mad. Seena was presently very, very mad.

"Yes, good for him," she said again, "for coming out of the closet like that. And in front of you, Daddy. Where did you corner him? On top of your beloved mountain? You can scare the bejesus out of anyone, Daddy, on a mountaintop or in this living room. I think that took a lot of guts on Junior's part."

Seena could say anything she wanted without fear of her father's wrath. She was his favorite daughter. He had always admired her spirit.

"And what do you think, Lizzie?" asked Mrs. Margaret Deco, attempting to bring her introverted daughter into the conversation.

"Doesn't matter to me what Junior is," mumbled Elizabeth Deco Brown, also known as Lizzie, the blah member of the family. Mrs. Brown, the middle Deco sister, wasn't pretty at all. She had tight, curly hair, and was called "pleasingly plump" by the family when in fact she was fat. Lizzie had a plain face, a double chin, close-set eyes, thin lips (a family trait), no personality whatsoever, and was practically mute. She rarely spoke.

Lizzie Deco had married someone exactly like herself, Dr. Maxwell Brown. Lizzie's husband was a fat, double-chinned individual more boring than his wife, if that was humanly possible. He wore bow ties and ill-fitting suits, had a paunch, and was exactly his wife's age, almost to the day. A large chunk of Dr. Brown's pants was constantly caught in the crack of his substantial behind.

Dr. Maxwell Brown was a proctologist. He came to life only when discussing proctological matters in the company of patients and other proctologists. The pair had one son, a twelve-year-old sissy. His name was Maxwell Brown, either the Third or Fourth. People tended to forget.

"'Doesn't matter to me.' What the hell kind of answer is that, Elizabeth?" boomed an irritated Arthur Deco Senior. "'Doesn't matter to me.'"

Considering the amount of conversation Lizzie Brown spoke every day, her sentence about Junior was fairly talkative. Lizzie never spoke unless spoken to. And then it was as few words as possible. It had been that way for Lizzie from grammar school through graduation from college. Present friends and former classmates of Mrs. Elizabeth Deco Brown wondered if she ever said anything filthy dirty to her husband.

"I . . . uh . . . I . . ." she stuttered, trying to respond to her father's assault. Arthur Deco Senior made Lizzie very nervous. All she ever wanted in life was his approval, which she never received. Lizzie was convinced her father disliked her so much because she was fat.

"Well, *I* don't think anything is good about my brother being a queer," hissed Mrs. Hattie Deco Strange. "He's gay, therefore he's a despicable misfit. I myself am mortified and ashamed that a brother of mine is a diseased homo."

"Hear, hear," snapped Senior, nodding his head in agreement.

"Well," said Mrs. Deco angrily, "I think both of you should be ashamed of yourselves. That includes you, Father. Talking about your own son that way. And Hattie, you should be ashamed too. That is no way to talk about your brother."

"Diseased?" said Seena. "Who's diseased? What are you talking about, Hattie?"

Hattie Strange, the oldest of the three Deco sisters, looked older than her twenty-six years. She had her father's mousy brown hair cut in bangs across her forehead and the rest in a pageboy. She possessed a nondescript body and stumpy legs. Hattie dressed conservatively in blazers, sweaters, skirts, and flat shoes.

She and her husband, Morgan Strange, a lawyer, were big shots in Bowling Green society, contributing generously to the Bowling Green Chamber Orchestra and the Bowling Green Symphony Orchestra. The pair were far more hateful and bigoted than most of the members of the Methodist church congregation they belonged to.

Hattie and Morgan Strange strongly believed women should not have a choice regarding the life or death of their fetus, Jews should not be allowed in any branch of the United States government, Negroes should not be allowed in the front of the bus, and gays should not be allowed to live.

"Diseased?" said Seena again. "Mother's right. How dare you say those terrible things about your own brother?"

"Well, faggots are full of disease," said Hattie. "It's a proven fact."

"Hattie," said Margaret Deco.

"What, Mother?"

"You keep using the word faggot. And I don't like it."

"I apologize, Mother, but that's what Junior is. He's . . . he's . . . a homosexual and God knows what else, and that's all there is to it. Junior is a disgrace to our family. Gay men are called queers because they *are* queer. To be a gay is a mortal sin. Even the Bible says so."

"Where does the Bible say being a homosexual is a sin?" asked Seena.

"It says homosexual behavior is abhorrent."

"Where? Where does the Bible say that?"

"It just does," said Hattie. Then turning to her father, she said, "I don't think Junior's being gay should ever leave this room. No one needs to—"

"You *can't* keep something like this secret," interrupted Margaret Deco. "It will get out. It's bound to. Someone in New York has already contacted us about Junior, not hiding their feelings one bit. It's bound to get bandied about Bowling Green sooner or later."

"What is, Mother?" asked Elizabeth Deco Brown, trying to appear interested.

"That your brother's gay," explained Mrs. Deco.

"Oh," said Lizzie.

"Well, we don't have to *help* spread the story, Mother," argued Hattie. "I mean, I don't want Morgan to know, or my boys, or—"

Seena stood up and started out of the room.

"Where are you going?" growled her father.

"I'm going for a walk, Daddy. Hattie's bullpucky is making me nauseous." Seena stopped walking and turned to her father. "Daddy, you and Hattie should be ashamed of yourselves. Talk about a mortal sin. Abandoning Junior, in my mind, is a mortal sin. We must all stay by his side. Every one of us. You, Daddy, especially. You should *not* abandon your son, nor you, Hattie, your brother, because he admitted he's gay. You all should be ashamed of yourselves if you do. But I'll tell y'all this. I'm not abandoning him, no matter what's decided in this room."

Seena Deco walked out of the living room.

"Seena's absolutely right," said Margaret Deco, after she had gone.

"Seena's not right, Mother," said Hattie Strange. "Seena is wrong."

"Junior is our son and your brother," said Margaret Deco slowly and softly. "We *must* stay by his side. We . . . are . . . a *family*. We cannot abandon the boy."

"He is not a boy, Mother, he is a man," said Arthur Deco Senior. "He is seriously sick, Mother. Mentally, I mean. I fully agree with Hattie on this matter, though I am not sure what the solution is."

"All the more reason we should stand behind Junior," said Margaret Deco.

"Why's that, Mother?" asked Hattie.

"Because, as your father just said, Junior's seriously sick."

"That's not what Daddy meant, Mother. Daddy meant—"

"Do *not* start explaining what I mean, Hattie. You hear?" said Senior.

"Sorry, Daddy. Anyway, as I said before, our Bible renounces homosexuality. Good Christians are *not* homos. If Junior had shot someone to death it wouldn't be as heinous as being the sick, perverted animal he is. If Junior had killed a gay person I *definitely* would have stood by his side."

"I'm surprised at you, Hattie," said Margaret Deco.

"I'm sorry, Mother," said Hattie Deco Strange. "You all can stay by Junior's side, but as far as I'm concerned, Junior's not my brother anymore."

Then she too left the room.

"I agree with Hattie," said Arthur Deco Senior.

"Junior is your son, Father."

"I know that, Mother, but that's the way I feel," he said angrily.

"Well, I refuse to disown my son, and if—"

"And that's not all, Mother," interrupted Senior. "Junior transferred ten million dollars from his trust fund to this Cotton man."

"He transferred *ten million dollars*? To his . . . his . . . room-mate?" said Margaret Deco. "How do you know?"

"Sidney told me."

"Can Junior do that?"

"Apparently," said Senior, obviously discouraged.

2

Arthur Deco Junior received his pilot's license at the end of March. His father still bought him his new plane as promised. This surprised Junior. He thought after his gay confession, his father would have nothing to do with him. Art wondered why his father was being so generous. It didn't make any sense at all.

In June Art flew by commercial airline to the Cessna plant in Wichita, Kansas, to pick up his plane. Art didn't ask Eddie to accompany him. It was just as well. Before Art could get the words *Eddie, you hate to fly. Why don't you stay home?* out of his mouth, Eddie said, "I hate to fly. Why don't I stay home and meet you at Teterboro when you return?"

"Good idea," said Art.

In Wichita, when Art Deco saw the actual plane, he gulped with delight. The aircraft, a brand-new Cessna T182, all spanking shiny new, was far more beautiful standing there in front of the hangar than all the pictures his father had shown him.

The single-engine aircraft could hold three passengers and the pilot easily. The individual pilot's and copilot's seats (if it was necessary to have a copilot) and the two passenger seats in the rear of the plane were covered in a rich, polished camel-colored leather.

The aircraft had a sleek white body with colorful blue stripes running along both sides of the fuselage from its tail to the front of the plane's nose. The plane had three wheels, one up front and one on each side of the fuselage. The wheels were enclosed in wheel pants. The plane was light blue with white stripes on both sides of the fuselage.

Art's salesman, a plump, fleshy guy, had a red drinker's face and a stomach that hung over his belt. He wore a dress shirt buttoned tightly around his neck, the points of which were turned upward. The salesman's tie was knotted unevenly, with the thin part hanging down lower than the fat part. Hugh Jones was the salesman's name, but he preferred to be called Jonesy. Jonesy was one of those perpetual frat boys whose body and heart never left dear ol' Sigma Chi. Nor did his intellect. Jonesy offered Junior "a glass of bubbly" before Art took off for New York City. Junior declined the salesman's offer.

"One glass of champagne won't hurt you," said fat, veiny-nosed Jonesy. "Besides, there aren't any cops up there to pull you over."

Then Jonesy laughed hysterically. Jonesy was still laughing when Art walked out of his office to do a preflight check before he took off. Art circled the plane alone for his first official check. He did the cockpit check by himself too. Jonesy wanted to sit beside Junior during the cockpit check, but Art waved him off. He didn't want the smell of champagne in the cockpit. Jonesy stood on the tarmac, the champagne bottle in one hand, the two empty glasses in the other, in what appeared to be a funk.

Sitting behind the wheel of his brand-new Cessna, wearing his Loro Piana brown leather jacket and his Tom Ford sunglasses (two recent purchases for Art's maiden flight), Art Deco never felt better in his entire life. When Art was satisfied everything checked out, he gave Jonesy the thumbs-up sign. The salesman produced a weak smile in return. Art started the prop, rolled out to the runway, checked for clearance, and took off.

Art Deco did not fly to the Teterboro, New Jersey, airport, where Eddie Cotton waited worried to death, pacing nervously back and forth. He flew instead to the Westchester, New York, airport, where the architect and model Tim Duncan was expecting him. While Duncan got himself settled into Art Deco's new plane, Junior telephoned Eddie Cotton at Teterboro and told him he was never coming back to Eddie. Art said he and Tim Duncan would be away for about a month. Eddie could stay in the apartment until a week before they got back. If Eddie was still there when Art and Tim returned, Art would have Eddie Cotton evicted. Art Deco told Eddie Cotton he would give him a heads-up before they returned.

Art and Tim flew to Prince Edward Island in Newfoundland, where the two new lovers enjoyed their honeymoon. The pair vacationed for more than three weeks. They stayed at the isolated but cozy Johnson Shore Inn on the Gulf of St. Lawrence, and ate many times at a restaurant named Flex Mussels. The two fished and clammed and made love the entire time they were there.

3

Eddie Cotton was shattered.

He never budged from the living room couch in Art Deco's apartment. He sat, ate, and slept there. Sometimes he said aloud, "That fucker. That little fucker." Otherwise he sat in silence. He hardly ate. He drank a lot of wine, and nodded off now and then.

On the morning of the third day, Eddie jumped up, shaved, dressed in decent clothes, found his bankbook, and took a taxi to the branch he and Art always went to. Eddie stood in a long line of customers, a nervous wreck, not knowing why he felt that way. When his turn came, he asked to see what his savings account balance was.

"Your name?" asked the teller.

"Eddie Cotton."

"Do you have proof you're who you say you are?"

"I have my driver's license."

"Could you please show it to me?"

Eddie dug his wallet out of his back jeans pocket and produced his driver's license. The clerk took his time looking at Eddie's license.

"I'm in sort of a hurry," said Eddie Cotton.

"Your PIN number," said the clerk.

"Six three two nine."

"Don't tell me," yelled the clerk. "Put it in the box next to you."

Eddie Cotton looked at the bank clerk and started to see the exploding fireworks in his head. He hadn't seen them for a while. "Don't you *ever* yell at me again, you hear, you puny little fuckhead?" he said, bouncing his index finger off the bulletproof glass. The customers at the adjoining windows turned to look at the angry man.

Eddie pushed the numbers into the small black box.

"Hit ENTER, please," said the shaken bank teller.

Eddie hit ENTER.

"Edward Cotton?" asked the bank teller.

"Yes."

"You have a zero bank balance, Mr. Cotton."

"A zero bank balance?"

"That joint account was closed over a month ago by a Mr. Arthur Deco Junior," explained the teller, "and all the money transferred to another account."

"What account?"

"I am not permitted to say," said the bank clerk.

"That's not possible, is it? How can someone take my money?"

"It was a joint bank account, sir. The other party of the joint account can do whatever he wants with the money," explained the teller.

Eddie Cotton walked out of the bank. He was broke. Also, in a few weeks he would be homeless. He didn't want to think about it.

4

Three weeks later Eddie Cotton decided to bite the bullet and leave Art Deco's plush duplex apartment. Having to go was hard, but what else could he do? Art had given Eddie an ultimatum. *Be out before we get back or I'll have you evicted.* They would be back in two days. Eddie Cotton couldn't face the embarrassment of being there when the two arrived. Or being evicted. But he didn't have a penny to his name. He couldn't even afford the McBurney YMCA. He'd have to go home to Flushing. He looked for and found the maid's expense money. At least he could use that for taxi fare.

It was embarrassing to call for the dolly to take his bags down to the front of the building. Every apartment house employee knew he was being thrown out of Deco's plush duplex for a new lover. Eddie figured Saffeiodi, the concierge, was the big-mouth who was spreading the word. The concierge had never liked Eddie.

Eddie took a taxi to the corner of his street in Flushing, but couldn't walk into his house. Not yet. He thought he'd grab a cup of coffee first at the neighborhood pizza parlor and go over his story again, except the neighborhood pizza parlor was gone. Everything had changed. Flushing, New York, looked like Seoul, Korea. Where there used to be pizza parlors, grocery stores, and stands selling flavored ices, there were now Korean restaurants, Korean pastry shops, and Korean bodegas.

So Eddie went home.

"I missed you guys somethin' terrible," he told his parents. "I was real homesick, is what it was. I came home because I was real homesick."

"Poor boy," said his teary-eyed mother.

Eddie knew that's what his mother wanted to hear, how homesick he was. She'd make everything okay if he kept telling her that.

"What happened to the wonderful job you had? And your wonderful apartment?" asked Eddie's suspicious father. Sal Cantelone wondered when this son of his was going to get the hell off his back. Didn't sons leave home and unmarried daughters stay and help their mothers with the housework? Wasn't that the way it was supposed to work?

"I quit that job, Papa. You mind if I stay here for a while, Mama, an' try to figure things out?"

"Of course I don't mind," said Mama Cantelone. "You can stay as—"

"So," interrupted Papa Cantelone, "how long is all this figurin' out gonna ta—"

"Don't worry, sweetie," interrupted Mama Cantelone. "*This* is where you belong and this is where you'll stay. Forever, if you have to. Right, Papa?"

"Yeah. Sure," said Sal Cantelone, seeing his son for the lazy slug he was.

Eddie explained it had been hard to quit his great job and leave his incredible Park Avenue apartment to come home. "But let's face it," he added. "I was homesick. Plain, stupid homesick."

Eddie explained how he had to sell his fabulous sports car at a loss to make it possible for him to cover the penalties he had to pay to give up his apartment.

"What kinda penalties?" asked Eddie's father.

"Just penalties," said Eddie, wondering if he was keeping his stories straight. "Apartment penalties. Car penalties. Penalties I owed in Los Angeles. But Mama, I was *really* homesick," he whined.

"Poor boy," said Eddie's mother for the umpteenth time. "See, Sal? Didn't I tell you Eddie would be homesick? Didn't I tell you, Sal?"

"Yeah, yeah. You told me. You told me. So, Eddie, why'd you leave Los Angeles? You were doing so well out there."

"Like I said, I got homesick."

"You said you went to New York because of a better job or somethin'," persevered Sal Cantelone. "So what happened?"

"I got homesick in New York too," said Eddie angrily. "By the way, I'm busted," he added, changing the subject.

"*Busted*?" said Eddie's father. "You don't have any savin's from those terrific jobs you had?"

"I told you, Papa, I had to pay all those penalties."

"What goddamn penalties?"

"Calm down, Sal," said Sophie Cantelone. "It's not good for you to get so excited."

"An don't you have money left from the sale of your sports car?" asked Sal Cantelone. "Why did you have to sell your sports car in the first place? Why didn't you just drive it here to Flushing?"

"Yeah. Right," said Eddie, glaring at his father, pissed to the gills with all his dumb-ass questions. "I'd have to get a garage for the car, Papa. I couldn't leave a car like that out on the streets, could I? And garages cost a fuc— cost a fortune."

"Salvatore, Eddie's right," said Mama Cantelone. "He couldn't leave an expensive car on the street. Not in this neighborhood. That don't make sense."

"Right. Right," said Eddie's father, thinking Eddie was lying like a rug. "But you should still have some money left from sellin' the car, right?"

"Wrong, Papa. I ain't got nothin' left."

"How come?" persisted Eddie's father.

"Penalties," said Eddie Cantelone.

"There he goes with his fuckin' penalties again. Jesus Christ Almighty—"

"Calm down, please, Salvatore. This is bad for you. Bad."

Sal Cantelone glowered at his son.

Eddie hugged his mother again. "Jesus, it's good to see you, Mama."

"Don't you worry about money, my little baby boy," said Eddie's mother. "You'll be fine right here where you belong. I told you to stay here with me when you talked about movin' away. I told you you'd be homesick. Didn't I say that, Sal? Didn't I say Eddie would be homesick?"

"Yeah, yeah, you said it already," confirmed a very annoyed Salvatore Cantelone. This, he mused, was not gonna be a good day.

"We'll give you some spendin' money," said Mama Cantelone, "until you get yourself settled, won't we, Papa? We'll do that, won't we?"

Sal Cantelone said nothing.

"Great, Mama. Thanks, Papa."

So, thought Eddie Cotton to himself, maybe this wasn't such a bad idea after all.

He smiled, holding his mother to his chest.

5

A week later, Salvatore Cantelone woke Eddie out of a sound sleep.

"What time is it, Papa? Why ain't you at work?"

"Twelve noon's what time it is. And I ain't at work 'cause I ain't at work."

"Is everything okay?" asked Eddie, worried. "Is Mama okay? Where's Mama?"

"She's at the grocery store. She's shopping."

"So what's up, Papa?"

"I'll tell you what's up. I want you to get your lazy ass outta here and find yourself a job. I'll give you a fuckin' week to find a job or I'll break every bone in your body. Or get someone to do it for me, understand?"

That afternoon, Eddie bought *The New York Times* from the corner candy store, pulled the want ads section out, and threw the rest of the newspaper in a corner trash receptacle. He went back to the house and sat at the dining table circling job opportunities with a red Sharpie.

The next morning Eddie woke early, bought a cup of coffee at the deli, and drank it on a windy street corner. When Eddie finished his coffee he threw the empty coffee cup into an overflowing trash receptacle, and caught a Number 7 subway into center city. Eddie Cotton was packed in with the rest of the morning rush-hour crowd. He hung from a strap pressed against two construction workers hanging from the same strap.

Life changes, don't it? mused Eddie Cotton while holding his strap, swinging from side to side. A coupla months ago I was travelin' around in a chauffeur-driven Bentley. Now I'm takin' subways lookin' for work, sandwiched between two poor fuckin' bohunks. And whose fault is it?

Art Deco's fault, that's who.

I was always the nice one. I tried to better myself to please him. I took care of him. Yeah, I owed him. He gave me a lot, and I'll always be grateful for that. But the bastard deserted me, left me penniless and homeless, for Christ's sake. I never cheated on him or played him for a sucker. I *loved* the bastard. I really did, and look what he did to me. Cheated me out of the money he promised me, then threw me out on the street.

And then Eddie Cotton had a great idea.

He grinned, even though those little red fireworks were going off again in his head.

6

About the same time Eddie Cotton was riding that early morning subway into New York, Hattie Deco Strange was having breakfast with her father at his mansion in Bowling Green, Kentucky.

"Why was it so important to have this breakfast with me at this hour, Hattie?"

"Because," said Hattie Strange, "this is the time you have breakfast, and I wanted to tell you that I'm going to New York as soon as I can to talk to Junior."

"You had to tell me that at seven in the morning? Couldn't you have called me at the office to tell me that, and let me read my newspaper in peace? And what good do you think talking will do?" asked Senior, never taking his eyes off his two eggs over and bacon.

"Probably no good at all. But I wanted to talk to you about what I planned to do—"

"Do?" Arthur Deco looked at Hattie.

"What I planned *to say* to Junior. I wanted to get you alone. And I figured—"

"So talk." Hattie gave Senior a pain in the neck with her perseverance crap.

"Well, okay. It's about this thing that Art has. I just—"

"It's not a *thing*. It's . . . it's . . . something else."

"Like what, Daddy? A gene?"

"Yes. A gene," said Senior, still looking at his eggs.

"My God," said Hattie Strange, "that's worse, and scarier."

"Listen," said Arthur Deco Senior, looking up from his eggs for the first time. "I know how you feel, and I'm as upset as you are. I just don't want to upset your mother, so I keep my fury to myself when I'm around her. And you should do the same thing. Besides, what do you think you'll accomplish by chatting with your brother?"

"I'm not going to have a 'chat.' I'm going to read him the riot act," she said.

"What good do you think that will do? The riot act. Change his lifestyle? Besides, he never liked you very much. He always thought you were a huge pain in the ass."

"He did, did he? Thought I was a pain in the ass. Well, I—"

"Everyone in the family does."

Hattie went silent.

"Except me . . . and . . . uh . . . your mother," mumbled Senior.

Arthur Deco Senior sat at the head of the dining room table. Hattie Deco Strange was to his immediate left. She was facing the dining room window, which overlooked stately magnolia trees and rolling hills off in the distance.

Kentucky has such beautiful countryside, Hattie thought.

It was the first pleasant thought she'd had since she heard her brother was gay. Hattie pushed her scrambled eggs around her plate with her fork. Her father ate every last crumb of his fried eggs and bacon.

"This thing with Art really upsets me, Daddy. No, *scares* me. I cannot believe a member of our family is a goddamn pansy. I'm afraid my boys will . . . will . . ."

"Will what?"

"Will *catch* it."

"Being gay isn't contagious."

"How do you know? If it's a gene like you say it is, maybe one of my boys has the gene already. Maybe you passed the queer gene on to—"

"Goddamn it, I did no such thing," said Senior.

"But Daddy, don't all queers have AIDS? God, I would die if one of my boys caught AIDS from my goddamned brother. I'll absolutely kill that bastard brother of mine."

"Damn it, be quiet, Hattie."

"*Now* what are you buzzing Diana for, Daddy? Haven't you eaten enough?"

"No, I haven't eaten enough. I want a piece of French toast."

"Well, I see this god-awful mess hasn't affected your appetite, Daddy."

"Nothing ever affects my appetite," said Senior.

An elderly white woman came into the dining room, dressed in a black dress and a white apron, and said, "Sir?"

"Another piece of French toast, please, Diana."

Diana nodded and returned to the kitchen.

"I'm going to New York anyway, Daddy. Maybe a sisterly chat can do—"

"Do what?"

"*Some*thing. And if that doesn't work, maybe I'll . . . I'll . . ."

"What? Shoot him?"

"Maybe," said Hattie Deco Strange, very quietly.

"You better not," said Arthur Deco Senior.

There was silence in the Deco dining room. Then Hattie Strange said, "When are you flying up to New York again, Daddy? I really have to do some shopping."

"I'm flying up the day after tomorrow for a business meeting. If you really want to go to do some shopping you can come with me tomorrow."

Hattie Strange could hardly contain herself. She was delighted. She clapped her hands, silently, several times under the table and said, "Thank you, Daddy."

Now she could take her husband's .38-caliber snub-nosed Smith & Wesson revolver with her and not worry about airport security. They never bother checking passengers on private planes. She would carry the gun in her Hermès alligator Kelly bag. Hattie Deco Strange stood and kissed her father on his cheek.

He harrumphed.

FIVE

THE

MURDER

I

Arthur Deco Junior was lying on his back extremely dead.

The body had been found in the late afternoon of July 12, 2003.

The 911 telephone call had come in to police headquarters at 4:38 that afternoon. The caller had discovered a dead man in the living room of an apartment at East Eighty-third Street and Park Avenue.

"It might be a suicide," said the caller.

The first to respond to the 911 call were a pair of cops in a patrol car. They made the scene by 4:32 in the afternoon. Four more police cars arrived between 4:55 and 5:00 that evening. The five police cars parked in front of the expensive East Side Park Avenue apartment building forced taxis and automobiles to travel in a single lane past the prestigious address.

By the time the medical examiner, Dr. Meyer O'Tool, entered the apartment, at 5:10 that evening, the living room was a functioning crime scene. Yellow police tape had been pasted on the apartment's front door and across the entrance of the living room to protect the apartment from unwanted intruders. Two police officers stood guard at the apartment's entrance. A crime-scene photographer went about his business snapping photographs of areas he felt were important. Everyone inside the apartment was wearing plastic slip-ons over their shoes, plastic berets over their hair, and rubber gloves. Some wore white doctor's coats, though they weren't doctors.

A police lieutenant named Eddie Roach and a pretty but hard-looking rookie detective named Jackie Hallerhan arrived at the apartment building at 5:20 in the evening.

"You're late, Eddie," said the medical examiner, a longtime friend of the lieutenant's. "We've all been here for hours."

"Traffic," said the lieutenant.

"Got a siren?" asked the ME.

"Yes, and I used it, Meyer, but you know as well as I do that no one should ever get sick, commit suicide, or get murdered in Manhattan during the evening rush hour. Sirens aren't worth the noise they make between five and six o'clock in center city. So what's your guess?"

"I'd say there's a three-hour window starting an hour ago."

"That would take it back to anywhere from roughly two-ten, two-fifteen, to four-twenty this afternoon, right?" asked Detective Hallerhan.

"Right," said Dr. O'Tool. "I'll have a more exact time when I get the body back to my place."

"Give me a half hour, Meyer," said Lieutenant Roach, "and you can take it."

2

Deco lay on his back, arms and legs flung out from his sides. He had been found on the large living room floor of his apartment by his roommate. Deco's body was lying under a big front window overlooking Central Park. A black Beretta 9mm automatic was in his open right hand. Arthur Deco Junior was dressed in a black T-shirt, blue jeans, no socks, and Birkenstock sandals. His right sandal was on the floor near his bare right foot. Arthur Deco Junior had been shot above his right ear. The right side of his head was a mess. Blood from the wound stained the expensive Persian rug that covered the entire living room floor.

"The vic apparently shot himself through his right temple," said a woman from the Crime Scene Unit. "The bullet exited just above the vic's left ear and burrowed itself into the wall over there. This shell casing was on the floor beside the body." The CSU lady held up a clear plastic bag with the shell casing inside. "I'm pretty sure the bullet in the wall came from the gun on the floor. We'll send the casing to ballistics and get a report on it. Who wants it?"

"Me, please," said Detective Jackie Hallerhan. "I caught the case."

"By the way," said the CSU lady, "we found the front door unlocked and partially open."

The two detectives looked at each other.

"That's odd," said Hallerhan.

Lieutenant Roach shrugged his shoulders, then asked the roomful of technicians if anyone on the scene had found a suicide note from the dead man.

No one had.

"You might want to speak to his roommate," said one of the CSU people. "He's sitting over there."

The two detectives walked across the room to a good-looking young man sitting in a chair sobbing into his hands.

"I'm Detective Hallerhan. Who are you?" said Jackie Hallerhan, lifting her badge, which hung from a chain around her neck, and sort of shoving it into the face of the man sitting in the chair.

The man stood up. He was quite tall. He had red, watery eyes. "I'm Tim Duncan," he said. "I'm Art's . . . I mean, I *was* Art's . . . uh . . . I found him. I called 911 and reported the suicide."

"I'm Lieutenant Roach and this is Detective Hallerhan," said Eddie Roach, looking at his partner sternly. His eyes said, *Easy, Jackie.* "Would you like to sit down, Mr. Duncan?"

"No, thank you, sir. I'm fine."

Jackie Hallerhan got Eddie's message and said, much more sympathetically, "Did Mr. Deco leave any kind of note, Mr. Duncan?"

"No ma'am," said Duncan. "I looked everywhere. Mainly because it was such a surprise. I just wondered why . . . I mean why would he . . . I mean . . . Art was always such a happy person. He was always up. I just *hate* saying *was*." Tim Duncan sat down and began sobbing again.

"You couldn't find any note?" asked Eddie Roach.

"No sir. Nothing," Tim said, trying desperately to stop crying.

Detective Hallerhan said, "Was your roommate depressed about some—"

"No," interrupted Duncan, looking at the detective crossly. "I just *said,* he was a happy guy."

"Do you know of anyone who might have been his enemy, who may have wanted to kill him?" asked Lieutenant Roach.

"Yes," said Tim Duncan. "I certainly do."

"Who?" said Eddie Roach.

"His father."

"His *father,*" said Jackie Hallerhan.

"Yes, his father," repeated Tim Duncan. "His father is a rabid homophobe, I mean the worst kind, among other things. So's Art's sister Mrs. Hattie Strange. She hates gays as much as her father, maybe *more* than her father. By the way, she was up here today, the sister. Hattie."

"She was?" said Detective Hallerhan.

"So was his former lover, Eddie Cotton. Both would make excellent suspects, I should think."

"We'll be the judge of that," said Hallerhan.

"'Among other things'?" said Detective Roach. "What did you mean by that?"

Tim Duncan looked blankly at the lieutenant.

"You said Deco's father was a homophobe . . . *among other things.* What did you mean by 'among other things'?"

"What I meant was that Senior's anti-black, anti-Semitic, anti-everything," replied Duncan. "So's Art's sister, Mrs. Strange. Those two hate just about everything that isn't white, straight, American, and Christian."

"Did the victim's father and sister know the deceased was gay?" asked Lieutenant Roach.

"Yes."

"Did they know the victim was living with you, and—I presume—you're gay too?" asked Eddie Roach.

"The Deco family knew their son was gay, and I assume they didn't like it," said Duncan. "I'm not sure they knew their son was living with me yet."

"How's that?" asked Roach.

"I'm not sure Art told them," said Tim Duncan. "I'm . . . I was just moving in. I didn't even have a chance to make a key yet. Eddie Cotton had been living with Art for a couple of years before me. I'm pretty sure the family knew about him."

"One last thing," said Lieutenant Roach. "Why did you say Hattie Strange and Eddie Cotton would make excellent suspects?"

"Well, sir, Hattie Strange is a world-class homophobe. That's a pretty good reason, from my point of view. And as far as Cotton's concerned, I'm sorry to say Art did some nasty things to Eddie. He left him high and dry and without a cent to his name and kicked him out of this apartment. I think Art handled breaking off with Eddie Cotton in a terrible way, leaving him stranded at Teterboro Airport like he did. Will that be all, Lieutenant? I'm kind of tired."

"Thank you, Mr. Duncan," said Lieutenant Roach. "That will be all."

"Oh, and one other thing," said Tim Duncan, starting to sit, then standing. "This may or may not be import—"

"What, Mr. Duncan?" interrupted Hallerhan impatiently.

"Art was left-handed," said Duncan.

"So?" Hallerhan asked.

"So, Detective Hallerhan, the gun is in the vic's *right* hand," explained Lieutenant Roach. "A left-handed person wouldn't normally shoot himself with his right hand." Then, to Tim Duncan, "Thank you, Mr. Duncan, for the observation. It was a *very* important one."

3

Jackie Hallerhan had only been a detective for a month. She had been in a patrol car before that. For three years working the midnight to eight a.m. shift. In her early thirties, attractive, and on the tall side, Jackie wasn't married. She lived with her mother. The detective didn't want to live with her mother, but she did. Economics.

Jackie Hallerhan made detective by taking a bullet in her shoulder and still making an arrest. She had chased two robbery suspects down a subway entrance to the platform where she was shot. Though hurt and bleeding profusely, Jackie continued her pursuit, wounding one of the two purse snatchers. The other surrendered. Just after backup officers arrived, Jackie Hallerhan collapsed. She was taken to Lenox Hill Hospital, where doctors operated on her shoulder.

When she was released from the hospital, Jackie was promoted to detective and partnered with Roach. Jackie fell in love easily. She was a wee bit in love with her supervising lieutenant, Eddie Roach, a confirmed bachelor.

Lieutenant Roach was pushing fifty-one, with more than twenty-seven years' time on the force. He was a rumpled, balding, heavyset guy who hadn't done a lick of exercise in years, and looked it. Being the squad commander, it was the veteran Lieutenant Roach's job to supervise the rookie detective Jackie Hallerhan. The veteran and the rookie, barring some tough moments, liked each other.

Eddie Roach was aware Jackie Hallerhan needed a lot of sorting out and calming down. Jackie was a badger. When Jackie Hallerhan was a cop on the beat, she was known around the Nineteenth Precinct as one tough cookie. Roach knew Hallerhan had to learn to make her witnesses warm to her, rather than badgering them. She had to be taught you get more flies with honey than with vinegar when questioning a witness. Lieutenant Eddie Roach had a feeling deep down in his bones that Jackie Hallerhan would become an excellent detective . . . eventually.

"Don't suicides usually leave notes?" Hallerhan asked her lieutenant. "And aren't suicides usually depressed?"

"Yes to both," answered Eddie Roach. "But not always."

"So, Eddie, where do we go from here?"

"Downstairs to talk to the concierge."

4

The two detectives went to the apartment building's lobby to question the concierge; a loudmouthed guy named Mike Saffeiodi. Saffeiodi wore a black tuxedo, a black bow tie, a heavily starched white shirt, and a black cummerbund. Neither the cummerbund nor the belt could hold back Saffeiodi's beer belly. The belly kept Saffeiodi a good half foot away from the reception counter.

"Name's Mike Saffeiodi," said the concierge. "I'm workin' a double shift today. I been here since eight o'clock this mornin', an' I'm *still* here."

"Good for you," said Detective Hallerhan, who didn't like Saffeiodi on sight.

Lieutenant Roach knew that what the detective had just said wouldn't sit well with Saffeiodi.

"Mike, I'm Lieutenant Roach and this is Detective Hallerhan. We'd like to ask you a couple of questions, if we may."

"Ask away."

"First of all," said Roach, "has anyone been to visit Mr. Arthur Deco Junior today?"

"Yeah, a few people. I'll check it out for you in a minute. So how did you guys find out about the killin'. Someone call 911?" asked the concierge.

"Yes, someone called 911," said Lieutenant Roach.

"Who called?"

Jackie Hallerhan looked daggers at Saffeiodi for asking his damn questions, and at Eddie Roach for answering them.

"The call came from a man named"—the patient and amiable Lieutenant Roach checked his notebook—"Tim Duncan, Mr. Deco's roommate."

"More like his lover," said the concierge with a smirk. "You think this Duncan fag was the murderer?"

Detective Hallerhan rolled her eyes at her partner, then said, "Hey, Safferelli, *we* ask the questions. *You* answer them."

"Yeah, yeah. Just curious. And the name's Saffeiodi, sweetheart," said the concierge, clearly not in love with Hallerhan.

"I'm not your sweetheart, Saffawhatever. Don't call me that again. Just answer the questions. So who went up to Deco's apartment?"

"I gotta think."

"Don't think. Look it up. You must have a log, right? Every apartment house has a log, right?"

"Yeah. Sure. I forgot all about the log. Jesus, how dumb can you get? It's you guys. No, it's *her*," said Saffeiodi, jerking a hitchhiking thumb at Hallerhan. "She's got me all rattled. I got the damn log right here. Give me a sec."

The concierge brought the log up onto the reception countertop, flipped over the log's brown cardboard cover and a few pages, and tracked the day's callers and deliveries with his forefinger.

"Here. Here it is," he said standing up straight, relieved that he had found it. "It was Mr. Cotton. He came by at three forty-five. I told him the door's open. Mr. Cotton used to live with Mr. Deco. Mr. Cotton was Mr. Deco's first lover boy, before Mr. Duncan."

"What time did Cotton leave the building?" asked Hallerhan.

"We don't mark down when they leave, though I noticed Mr. Cotton leavin' kinda fast. About ten minutes after he got here."

"Why did you tell this Cotton guy the door was open?" asked Lieutenant Roach.

"Because Mr. Deco called down earlier and tells me to tell Mr. Duncan he was gonna take a shower and that he was gonna leave the apartment door open in case Duncan comes while he was in the shower. Mr. Duncan doesn't have a key yet. Mr. Deco said—"

"What time did Mr. Deco call down about the door being open?" asked Lieutenant Roach.

"I didn't mark it down," admitted the concierge.

Hallerhan sighed loudly.

"Guess, Mike," said Lieutenant Roach.

"Maybe it was like twelve thirty, one o'clock?" said Saffeiodi. "I was out on a lunch break, but my replacement tells me the message I was to give to Mr. Duncan. Mr. Deco tells Drew, that's my replacement's name, he tells Drew that Mr. Duncan would be here between one and three or four o'clock, and that the door would be unlocked while he was in the shower. Mr. Duncan's the *new* lover. Mr. Cotton's the *old* lover."

"Yeah, yeah. You told us that already," said Hallerhan.

"I understand, Mike, why you would tell Duncan the apartment door was open," said Eddie Roach, "he lives there, but I *don't* understand why you told this Cotton guy the door was open. He doesn't live in that apartment anymore, does he?"

"No, he don't. But I tells him because, like I said, he *used* to live with Mr. Deco. Besides, it really don't matter if I tells him or not. Mr. Cotton's got a key."

The lieutenant nodded his head. He understood.

"So who came next?" asked Hallerhan.

The concierge checked the log. "Before Mr. Cotton came," said Saffeiodi, talking only to Roach, "Mr. Deco's housekeeper, Damaris, came. She's always the first to arrive. She gets here every mornin' at ten and leaves at two, like clockwork. Cotton arrived at . . . let's see . . . at three forty-five. By the way, I see Cotton get the hell outta the buildin' about ten minutes after he gets here."

"Yeah, you told us," started Hallerhan. "Anybody else come to see Deco after Cotton?"

"Yeah. Deco's sister," said Saffeiodi to Roach.

"What time?" asked Hallerhan.

"About four o'clock, roughly," said the concierge.

"*Roughly*?" said Hallerhan.

"Yeah, *roughly*," the concierge said crossly to Hallerhan.

"Don't you have the precise time in the log?" asked the detective.

"Yeah, I have it in the log."

"So what time does it say in the log?"

"It says four o'clock. *Roughly*," said Saffeiodi without looking at the log.

"What's the sister's name?" asked Hallerhan.

"Mrs. Strange. Hattie Strange," answered the concierge, talking to Lieutenant Roach. "She's Deco's sister."

"You told her to go right up too?" asked Hallerhan.

"Yeah, I told her to go right up too. I *recognized* her," said an angry and getting angrier Saffeiodi. The concierge didn't like anything about Hallerhan, especially her tone of voice. "I *knew* it was Mr. Deco's sister," he said to Lieutenant Roach. "I *know* the sisters. There're three of 'em. They all come and visit from time to time. They all have keys."

"Why would Deco give all his sisters keys?" asked Roach, speaking more to himself than the concierge.

"So that if they came into town," said Saffeiodi, "they could always use Mr. Deco's apartment to freshen up in, things like that. Providin' they knocked first, I guess."

"What time did the sister leave?" asked Hallerhan.

"About four-ten."

"About?" said Hallerhan.

"Yeah," said Saffeiodi, "*about*. She hustled outta here too. Like Mr. Cotton."

"Who came next, Mike?" asked Lieutenant Roach.

"Uh, let's see," said the concierge. "Mr. Duncan came next at four-thirty. He was carryin' several cartons and bags of belongin's. I think he was movin' in with Mr. Deco today. I yelled to him as he passed by that Mr. Deco left the apartment door unlocked. Duncan's a model for Calvin Klein. He usually poses naked, except for a pair of squeezers. You can see him on them Calvin Klein billboards.

"Anyways, Mr. Duncan walks up to me and asks why Mr. Deco left the door open. I says because he was goin' to take a shower and didn't want you to be locked out. I tells him it's probably locked by now. I also tells him a couple of other people went up to see Mr. Deco before Duncan arrived. He asks me who. I tells him Mr. Cotton was one, Mr. Deco's sister was another. He asks me which sister. I tells him Mrs. Strange. He says, 'Shit,' and walks away. I remember that real well, the part about him sayin' 'Shit' when I tells him Mrs. Strange had come and gone."

5

"I'm sure Mr. Duncan's Mr. Deco's new lover," said Saffeiodi to Lieutenant Roach. "*Was* his new lover, I should say, right, Lieutenant? Duncan's a really nice guy. Not like that arrogant dip-shit Mr. Cotton, pardon my French, Mrs. Hallerhan."

"It's Miss, and just go on talking, Saffawhatever," said Hallerhan.

"Saffeiodi," the concierge said stubbornly to Hallerhan. Then, to Roach, "This Cotton guy was still livin' with Mr. Deco when Mr. Deco met Mr. Duncan. Mr. Duncan did some sort of architect work on the side when he wasn't posin' in his squeezers for Calvin Klein. Or maybe he did the posin' on the side." The concierge laughed. "Anyways, that's how he started workin' for Mr. Deco, doin' some architect work on a house Deco bought out in the Hamptons somewhere."

"When was that?" asked Hallerhan.

"I don't know," answered the concierge.

"Guess," ordered Detective Hallerhan.

"A year? Less than a year, maybe six months ago, somethin' like that."

"So Eddie Cotton was living with Deco when Deco met Duncan?" asked Lieutenant Roach.

"Yeah. Like I said, Eddie Cotton was Deco's original lover."

"He was? I don't remember you saying that," said Hallerhan.

"Sayin' what?"

"Saying Eddie Cotton was Deco's *original* lover?"

"Didn't I say that before?"

"No."

"Didn't I say that Cotton had lived with—"

"No. You never said anything like that. Do you know for a fact that Cotton was Deco's *original* lover?" asked Hallerhan.

"No. Yeah. I think Cotton's Deco's fir—"

"I don't care what you *think*, Saffarelli," said Detective Hallerhan, "just what you *know*."

The fat concierge dove into a deep sulk. You could tell by his facial expression. He shoved his hands into his pants pockets and looked down at his shoes.

"Excuse us for a minute," said Lieutenant Eddie Roach to the concierge, and led Detective Hallerhan off to the side.

"I don't play good cop, bad cop, Jackie. Ease up on the guy. Stop badgering him. It's obvious you don't like him, but that's not helping us any."

"I'm *not* badgering him, Eddie."

"Yes, you are. Start calling him by his name and stop using Saffawhatever and Saffarelli. Use Saffeiodi. Or Mike. You're losing this guy, and I'm not happy about it. Not at all. In a couple of minutes he going to clam up because he's so pissed at you. We'll lose whatever information he may have had for us."

"He annoys the hell out of me, the macho asshole."

"Put it behind you, Jackie. And make it quick. Your damn attitude's getting in the way of his answers," said Lieutenant Roach angrily. "I don't like the way you're handling this *at all*. Stop it right now or you'll lose me as a partner, and I'll tell the cap why."

"Yes sir," said Hallerhan.

The two walked back to the concierge.

"Go on," said Lieutenant Roach.

"Like I was sayin'," said the concierge, still pouting, talking to just Lieutenant Roach, "Tim Duncan comes through the revolvin' doors with his arms loaded with cartons and packages a little before four-thirty. At least that's what I marked down here in the log."

Jackie was going to say *a little?* but changed her mind. "Do you mark everything down in that log . . . uh . . . Mike?" she asked nicely.

"Yeah, I do," said Saffeiodi, not looking at Jackie Hallerhan.

"Could you ever *not* mark something down, Mike?" asked Hallerhan.

"No. . . . Wait . . . Yeah," he said, talking to Detective Hallerhan. "When some visitor goes, leaves the buildin', we don't mark it down. We just sorta guess. We do that if someone asks us when did so-and-so leave, like you guys did."

"What I mean is, Mike," said Hallerhan, "can anybody get by you guys at the front desk without anyone marking it down?"

"Only if we're very busy, Detective. Or maybe if one of us is takin' a leak. Pardon the French, Detective Hallerhan."

"It's okay, Mike," said Jackie Hallerhan, disgusted but not showing it, smiling her fake smile that only Lieutenant Roach recognized.

"So what happened when Mr. Duncan came into the lobby?" asked Eddie Roach.

"Okay. So Albin Alkamon, the doorman here, runs outside and tries to help take some of Mr. Duncan's packages, but Mr. Duncan blows him off and heads for the elevator. When he walks by the desk here, I yells out to him, 'The door's open, Mr. Duncan.' An he says—"

"You told us this already . . . uh . . . Mike," said Hallerhan. She couldn't help herself.

6

Later that night the two detectives were having a couple of beers at the bar of Gino's Restaurant on Lexington Avenue between Sixty-first and Sixty-second Streets.

"Something about the Deco suicide bothers me," said Lieutenant Roach. "It just doesn't smell like a suicide. My bones keep telling me it's murder."

"Your bones generally know what's going on," said Jackie Hallerhan. "So what's bothering you in particular about this one, Eddie?"

"A bunch of things. For one, there wasn't a note. That's no big deal, but it's something. Also Deco's roommate said that Deco was generally a happy guy, so he wasn't depressed. Notes and a history of depression are generally good indicators of a suicide. For another, and a big one, the Beretta was by Deco's right hand and not his left. That's a biggie, Jackie. A left-handed person isn't going to shoot himself with his right hand. Even Deco's roommate . . . what's-his-name . . ."

"Tim Duncan."

"Yeah, even Duncan knew that. It just isn't natural. And here's another thing," said the lieutenant. "The gun was *in* Deco's hand. If someone shoots himself, the gun's not going to be in his hand after he falls. The gun's going to be on the floor somewhere, *not* in his hand. Maybe *near* his hand, but not in it. Know what I mean?"

"And maybe when the ballistics report comes back," said Hallerhan, "it'll show that the slug the CSUs dug out of the wall has a different fingerprint than the Beretta we found on the floor. That would be something else, wouldn't it?"

"That'd be nice, Jackie, but I wouldn't count on it," said Lieutenant Roach. "The shell casing the CSU folks found on the floor is most likely the casing from the bullet they'll dig out of the wall. The CSU person said basically the same thing. She said, if I remember correctly, that she was 'pretty sure' the casing on the floor was the casing for the bullet in the wall."

"Yeah, but Eddie, the CSU woman left some wiggle room. 'Pretty sure' doesn't mean 'for certain.'"

"Like I said, Jackie, don't get your hopes up about the ballistics report. But the gun in the guy's hand after he falls, *and* in his right hand when he's left-handed, now we're talking murder."

7

A week later at the precinct, early in the morning, the two detectives sat facing each other. They both had their feet up on their desks, angled to the side so each could see the other's face. They had their notebooks in front of them and were going over and over all the facts they knew about the Deco suicide/murder. They each had a Styrofoam cup of hot coffee that Jackie Hallerhan had just brought back to their desks.

"This coffee sucks the big one. It took me forever to get these too. There was a long line for this shit," said Jackie Hallerhan after she was seated.

Eddie Roach's mind was elsewhere. "While you were getting the coffee, the cap called me into his office."

"Yeah? What did he have to say?"

"He said we're closing the books on Deco."

"He said *what?* So fast? Why? We haven't even really gotten started investigating it," said a stunned Jackie Hallerhan.

"The cap figures the Deco case can be labeled a suicide and nobody will argue. So that's what the boss has suggested we do. Make it a suicide and get it off the precinct's books. The boss asked me if I would consider doing that, and being as I'm not one for banging heads with the cap, suicide it is."

"Jesus," said Jackie. "Did you tell Bigatel the vic's roommate said the vic was never depressed, and there wasn't a note? And wait . . . did you tell him not only the gun that the vic supposedly used to kill himself was in his wrong hand, *but* it wasn't even in his hand. I mean, did you tell Captain Bigatel those things, Eddie? So why do you guys want to drop the case?"

"*I* don't want to drop the case, Jackie, the precinct commander does."

"*Shee*-it," said Jackie Hallerhan.

"I told Bigatel everything. I told him my bones thought it was murder. I told him we haven't even received the ME's report yet. I told him all the stuff you just mentioned. But the cap just wants the case to go away. He said he's got too many legitimate murders he's responsible for right now. He said he won't get an argument from the DA about this being a suicide. He said it looks and feels like a suicide, and like I said, he's *suggesting* I make it a suicide and forget about it. Biggie said he doesn't need another murder to worry about, not with CompStat coming up in a week. Right now he just wants the Deco case to go away."

"Jesus," muttered Jackie Hallerhan.

"I even asked for more time, Jackie. Just a couple a more days. I told Joe if we couldn't come up with anything in forty-eight hours, then make it a suicide. But the cap refused to budge. He said, 'I want it off the precinct's books, and I want it off ASAP. He mentioned CompStat again. He said, 'I'd appreciate it, Eddie, if you made this happen.'"

"That's the problem with CompStat," muttered Hallerhan. "It

makes precinct commanders shove cases under the rug so they won't have to deal with them and get their asses reamed at CompStat."

"I suppose so, Jackie."

"You know something, Lieutenant?"

"What?"

"Someone's getting away with murder," said Jackie Hallerhan.

SIX

THE PRIVATE EYE

I

My name is Jimmy Netts and I'm a private eye.

My name wasn't always Jimmy Netts and I wasn't always a private eye. My name used to be Jimmy Nettlestein and I used to be a podiatrist. Most people don't even know what a podiatrist does. The word podiatrist comes from the Greek *pod,* or foot. I took care of peoples' feet. I have no idea where *iatrist* comes from.

Before becoming a podiatrist, I was a kid.

I was a thin child, susceptible to head colds. I had blond hair, no eyebrows (my eyebrows were too blond to see them), and a long nose. I was Jewish and shy. I was shy because I was Jewish. I was always afraid my schoolmates would find out I was Jewish and call me a kike. I wouldn't know what to do if they did.

I grew up in a Catholic neighborhood outside Philly. A place called Bala Cynwyd. Our house was in the shadows of St. Matthias Church. Thank God my parents didn't know or care about Jewish holidays. Because of their ignorance, I stayed in school during Rosh Hashanah and Yom Kipper, the holiest days in Judaism, and wasn't always taken for being Jewish. I could have almost passed for a Christian. I had white-blond hair. Unfortunately, my nose gave me away.

I got in fights a lot. I don't know why. I just did. Maybe I was annoying. I wasn't a good fighter. As a result, I had my two front teeth chipped once, and my nose broken twice. When the plastic surgeon set my nose the second time he also took the bump out of it.

That was the good news. My father was the bad news. He was a dentist. But cheap. My father wouldn't cap my two broken front teeth until I finished high school.

"Why do I have to wait five years, Dad?"

"Because caps are expensive. You'll get into another fight and break them again."

My father was wrong. I never got into another fight. But my front teeth remained chipped. Which gave me a complex. In my mind every girl I asked for a date stared at my two chipped front teeth, then said no.

Five years later, when I graduated high school, my father finally capped my two teeth. The caps looked great. My new teeth made me look handsome, almost. I had blond hair, a short nose, and two nonchipped front teeth.

While the cement was still drying on my new front teeth, I jumped out of my father's dental chair and went with a bunch of my friends to Ocean City, New Jersey. We were celebrating our high school graduation. We all put our bathing suits on in the car. When we arrived at the beach, we dashed out of the car, ran down to the ocean, and jumped in. I landed on top of someone. My teeth hit the top of that person's head and I broke my caps.

A few days after I graduated high school I was playing basketball in the schoolyard with fat Danny Endy. We were playing HORSE. I asked Danny if he was going to college. He told me he was going to go to Temple and become a podiatrist.

I asked, "Why?" and he answered, "Because podiatrists make a lot of money."

Eventually I went to Temple University and became a podiatrist too.

2

My sister and I were born and raised in Philadelphia.

My sister went to the University of Pennsylvania, and Temple University for her master's and doctorate degrees in art history. Then my sister became a teacher.

She saved her money and bought a small row house in a really scuzzy part of the city, down by the Schuylkill River. At the time my sister lived near the Schuylkill River it was the most polluted body of water in America. If you fell into the Schuylkill, all of your open cuts would immediately fester. Philadelphia colleges and universities recruited the dumbest students for their rowing teams. Only dummies would row on the Schuylkill River. One stupid sculler from the University of Pennsylvania's rowing team almost died from hepatitis contracted when he fell into the Schuylkill River. The Schuylkill seemed to be one big tainted clam.

Ten minutes after my sister bought her row house by the Schuylkill, the city began to clean up the river. Now the river's spotless. The water's as healthy as the spas in Baden-Baden. Maybe healthier. Rowers don't have to be simple-minded stupes anymore. Now they can be smart. They can fearlessly dip their oars into the Schuylkill River without worrying about catching any infectious diseases.

And then the Philadelphia Planning Commission decided to make the part of the city where my sister's row house was a metropolitan showcase. They gentrified that entire section of the city, and changed the neighborhood's name to Society Hill. When my sister had to sell her brownstone because of the offer she received of a full professorship at Western Kentucky University in Bowling Green, she made a fortune.

One should never tell a lady's age. So I'll just tell you mine. I'm forty-three, seven years younger than my sister. My sister never married. Why she never married is a short, tragic story. It goes like this. The man she was desperately in love with and engaged to drowned in a riptide in Atlantic City, New Jersey, two days before the wedding. My wife died two months and two days after we were married in an automobile accident. I loved her very much.

My sister and I never discuss matrimony, ever.

My sister's a pleasant-looking woman. As a matter of fact, everything about her is pleasant. She has a pleasantly round figure, a pleasantly round face, and a pleasant nature. She wears her hair short, with bangs. She dresses in capri pants, short jackets, and wears lots of colors, pink being one of her favorites. My sister is extremely intelligent. She's inclined to overlook the faults of others. She has a ton of energy but she's very calm. She's always neat as a pin and keeps a tidy house. She's known to curse if the spirit moves her, and she's not afraid to speak her mind when she wants to. She also has a gentle disposition, a great smile, is immensely loyal, and is adored by her students, her friends, her family, everyone.

As for me, on a good day I'm sometimes considered cute. On a bad day I'm not the greatest-looking guy walking. I'm much bigger now. My blond hair has turned black and curly. I wear glasses and have asthma that erupts when I get uptight. The asthma forces me to carry an inhaler.

3

My mother's name was Edith. Edith was a complainer. My father's name was Nathaniel. His friends called him Nate. Neither parent was anything to rave about. My sister and I never ever got any direction or advice from either one. The only things they gave us were our names.

My parents named me James Hirsch Nettlestein. My middle name was in honor of my great-grandfather, a much-revered Philadelphia rabbi, James Menachem Hirsch. They named Nettie Nettie because it went nicely with Nettlestein. Nettie Nettlestein.

Our parents are dead now.

My father married my mother for her money. My mother's father (my grandfather) owned "The Business" and was very wealthy. But right after my father married my mother, "The Business" took a turn for the worse (at least that's what my father was told) and suddenly my grandfather couldn't afford his new son-in-law. So my father continued being a mediocre dentist. When I was a kid, I was prone to nightmares about The Business. I was never sure what exactly The Business did. I thought The Business did something scary, like gathered up Chinese people and trucked them to The Business, where they were chopped up and sold as pork lo mein.

Uncle Bernie was the boss of The Business. He took over from my grandfather when Grandpop died. Uncle Bernie's dead now too.

A long time before he died, Uncle Bernie told me, "You don't have the *mazel* for The Business, son."

Uncle Bernie told me about my lack of *mazel* the day he took me for a ride in his long, hunter's-green, four-door Cadillac with the shiny chrome grille. He was taking me on a tour of his three cheesy retail stores in little towns near Philadelphia. While driving, Uncle Bernie ruffled the hair on the top of my head with his well-manicured right hand and called me "son" a lot. I wasn't his son, and I didn't like him calling me that. Or ruffling my hair.

It was during his hair ruffling that he told me that crap about not having enough *mazel.*

Eventually I learned what *mazel* meant and what the The Business did.

(Mazel means "smarts.")

The Business was a two-bit mens' clothing factory on Arch Street, in a run-down, really depressing section of South Philadelphia. I would have had to toil my entire life in that smelly, rat-infested dump, which had a really rotten smell, something quasi-redolent of dead mice trapped in walls. I would have wasted away my youth, middle, and old age cutting cloth from patterns to make mens' suits with my other *schnorrer* uncles.

(Schnorrer means one who habitually takes advantage of others' generosity.)

I would have been paid slave wages and I would have worked Christmas Day and New Years Day, and only had from Friday sundown until Saturday sundown and the Jewish High Holidays off. My Uncle Bernie was an Orthodox Jew.

Decades later, I recalled my uncle's advice about not having enough *mazel* and wondered if Bernie throughly disliked me and considered me a dumb clod who could never learn how to become a cutter in The Business.

Or was Bernie giving me a chance to run for my life?

I think he was telling me to run.

4

Nettie was an assistant professor at Temple when I decided I wanted to go there. She had to write a letter of recommendation for me to be accepted at the university. Another letter from Nettie got me into their medical school. Another letter, and I was admitted to the Temple University School of Podiatric Medicine, aka the university's School for Feet, located at Eighth and Race Streets. Good old Nettie. She's now a full professor of art history at Western Kentucky University in Bowling Green. Or did I mention that?

"Professor Nettie Nettlestein," I said to her at our celebration dinner at Bookbinder's Seafood Restaurant in Philly. They had the best oyster crackers at Bookbinder's. There were always a lot of them in a big bowl on every table.

"How 'bout that, Jimmy? I'm a full professor now," she said, taking a moment to relish the title. "I never thought I'd be a full professor."

"Why not?" I asked.

"I don't know."

We ate some oyster crackers and waited for the waitress to clear our dinner dishes away. Then Nettie suddenly said, "Come down to Bowling Green with me."

"*What!*"

"All you do is rattle around your apartment bored to death. Bored with people's feet, bored with your life, bored with everything. Plus you've always hated being a podiatrist, haven't you?"

"Yeah."

"So come down to Bowling Green with me. Maybe you'll meet a real pretty Southern belle down there who says y'all, and start a new life."

There was a big glob of silence, and then I said, "I don't think so, Nettie. They don't like Jews in the South."

"That's so not true," said my sister. "I'm going."

"You don't look Jewish, Nettie. Come on, what do you think the chances are of a Jewish podiatrist making it in Kentucky?"

"They *love* Jewish podiatrists in Kentucky."

When things weren't going Nettie's way, she made things up.

"Another thing, Nettie. Who would I root for down there? No Phillies. No Eagles. No Flyers. I don't know if they even play sports in Kentucky."

"I'm told they have pretty good basketball teams down there."

"Yeah, but they're colleges. I don't bet on colleges anymore. Just the pros."

"I just thought—"

"And I hear it's really clean in the South, Nettie, and that the people are very friendly and polite. Southerners have good manners. They say please and thank you, and wave a lot. They wave hello and goodbye to each other. Frankly, excessive waving gets on my nerves. I mean, who could cope with stuff like that? I'm a city boy, Nettie. I'm used to dirty, hostile, and rude, and not waving to everybody."

"Who told you all this crap?"

"I just heard it, Nettie. And what would I do down there? Start a new podiatry practice from scratch? Like I said, who would come to a Jew foot doctor in Bowling Green, Kentucky?"

I started to get this tightness in my chest. I felt around for my inhaler. I found it in my pants pocket and pumped some spray into my lungs.

"Relax, Jimmy. Just calm down. In the first place, you have this whole Jewish thing in your head. I don't know where you got it from. I haven't heard of any pogroms in Bowling Green, Kentucky, lately, have you? Maybe you get this Jewish thing from growing up next door to St. Matthias. But then, I grew up next door to St. Matthias and I don't have any of your Jewish *mishagas*."

(*Mishagas* means a mixed-up craziness in your head.)

"I think it's time you sold your damn podiatry practice," said my sister. "I really do. You've hated feet your entire life. You don't even like someone messing with *your* feet. Feet gave you your asthma. You never had asthma before you became a podiatrist, did you?"

"No."

"I bet you when you quit being a podiatrist you won't have asthma anymore."

"Possibly."

"So sell the damn practice, take whatever you get for it, and do something you like. You only go around once, you know."

"I'll get nothing for it."

"Isn't it better to be happy than rich?"

"I don't know. I've never been either."

"Okay, tell me this, Jimmy. If you had a chance to be anything you wanted to be, anything in the whole world, what would you be? I'm talking about your dream job. If you could do anything except be a pro quarterback, a movie star, or a rock star, what would you want to be?"

"A private detective," I said so quickly it amazed me.

"I thought that's what you'd say!" said my sister.

"Why did you think I'd say a private detective?"

"Because you've read just about every detective story ever written and you've seen every detective movie ever made. So be a private detective."

"I like the idea, Nettie, but there's two massive problems. One is, I don't know how to be a private detective. The other is, I would need a license and I don't know how to go about getting one."

"Oh, don't worry about those things," said Nettie. "I'll help you. I'm sure you can be a private detective *without* a license. I've heard most private investigators don't have licenses."

Like I said, my sister always based her facts on fitting her needs. And she was usually wrong, like she was wrong about saying most private detectives didn't have licenses.

"Listen, Nettie, I'm not so sure a Jewish private eye named Nettlestein in the South is such a good idea."

"Then don't be Jewish," she suggested. "Be Irish. A lot of private eyes are Irish, aren't they?"

"Yeah. But our name is Nettlestein."

"Then change it," said Nettie.

"To what? Jimmy O'Nettlestein?"

"How about Jimmy O'Netts?" Nettie asked.

"How about just Netts, then? Jimmy Netts?"

"Great!" boomed Nettie.

One can never fault Nettie's enthusiasm.

"So," I asked, "how do I start being an unlicensed private eye named Jimmy Netts?"

Nettie said, "When we get to Bowling Green, we'll find you a small office to rent. The office will have a front door that has a window in it with that funny opaque yellowish glass. In all the private detective TV movies we see, they always have offices with doors that have yellow opaque glass and a cheesy secretary in the waiting room. Won't that be fun, hiring a cheesy secretary? Do you know what opaque glass is?"

"No. But I know what a chee—"

"Very funny. Anyway, it doesn't matter. Just rent an office and I'll tell them what to do with the door."

There was a huge pause.

And then I said, "What'll I do about Hortense?"

5

Hortense was a dog I'd brought home from the pound. She was a little puppy then, and cute as a button. But then, all puppies are cute as a button. Hortense grew up to be ugly as hell. She was part whippet and part something else, probably anteater. She had skin tags and fatty tumors. Since Hortense became an adult, I grew to dislike her intensely. I should have gotten a pedigree Lab or golden pup. Those are my kinds of breeds. Those dogs look like dogs. Hortense looked like some kind of overgrown rodent.

"Maybe I should put her to sleep," I said to Nettie. "Neither one of us will miss her. I'll save a lot of money on vet bills. And I won't have to walk her at ten-thirty at night anymore. I can get in bed early if I feel like it. And—"

"You can't put Hortense down, Jimmy," said my sister gruffly. "No matter how much we dislike her, she's still a little creature with feelings."

"But she's old, Nettie."

"She not old enough."

Hortense was thirteen years old. She was a revolting dog who never did anything other dogs did. She never fetched, or carried the morning paper into the house, or chased a ball, or ran up to me with glee when I came home at night, or sat in my lap. If I tried to pick her up she would screech her bony ass off, something that sounded like, *"Rape!"* When I sat down on the couch next to her, she'd slink away. When I would go to pat the frigid old bitch's head, she'd duck as if my hand were filled with bubonic plague. Hortense wasn't even cute. But I couldn't put her to sleep. I guess I agreed with Nettie. Hortense was a little creature with feelings.

This much I'll say for old Hortense. She was a great athlete. Whippets are built for speed. The dogs are running machines. They're slim, with huge briskets, retractable ears, and skinny legs. They're the fastest dogs living. Maybe salukis are faster. I'm not sure. It's something to see whippets and salukis run. Both breeds can turn on a dime while running at forty-five miles an hour. All the better for catching rabbits and all kinds of small rodents. God didn't give whippets a thick coat of fur. He figured lugging a mackinaw around would slow the breed down. So He gave them sort of a light summer sweater. Makes sense.

Except in the winter.

Anytime the temperature dropped below sixty degrees I would have to put half a dozen sweaters on her. Hortense had fur, just not a lot of it. Sometimes, when it was below freezing outside, I would take Hortense for a walk with nothing on her, hoping the skinny old cur would catch pneumonia and die. But then I'd get two feet out the door and the damn dog would start to shiver. She'd look up at me with those big black eyes of hers. I'd turn right around and pull her back inside, put a couple of sweaters on her, and take her out again. I couldn't stand seeing her shiver, which surprised the hell out of me.

"You really don't want to put Hortense to sleep?" I asked my sister. "She's old and incontinent, and . . . and . . . she's never forgiven me for trying to dump her in the New Jersey marshes."

"I don't blame her, but we can't."

"Why not?"

"We just can't. So, Jimmy, come on, move down to Bowling Green with me."

"What if I get sick? They don't have any Jewish doctors in Kentucky."

6

During the summer of 2002, Nettie and I (and Hortense) moved to Bowling Green, Kentucky.

The town didn't impress me at first. Just a flat, hot, dusty hunk of land, with a big street running down the center of it called Scottsville Road. What *did* impress me were the many fast-food places where you could kill yourself quickly eating hamburgers, french fries, milk shakes, candy, and ice cream everywhere on Scottsville Road. There were Cracker Barrel, Steak 'n Shake, Wendy's, White Castle, McDonald's, and Brewster's Ice Cream, to name just a few. Eventually Scottsville Road ran by some fairly big, stately Southern homes with those mighty white pillars in front like Tara, Scarlett O'Hara's home in *Gone with the Wind*.

At first we thought of buying this nice house that had a weeping willow tree on the front lawn. The house was beside a river the locals called Drakes Creek. Drakes Creek looked a hell of a lot bigger than a creek to me, but then what does a city boy know about creeks? The house was beautiful and very big. So was the weeping willow guarding the front door. But the place was far too expensive for an ex-podiatrist-turned-private-eye and a university professor.

So we ended up buying a smaller house at 1645 Chestnut

Avenue. A sweet spinster named Elizabeta Dietrich had lived in that house her entire life, which was a long time, being that she died at one hundred on the nose. Elizabeta Dietrich was known around Bowling Green as Miss Elizabeta. We were told by the real estate agent, a chubby, middle-aged woman, that Miss Elizabeta had never married and had been as spry as a chicken when she died. The real estate agent, who I could tell hated Jews, hooted at the spry-as-a-chicken part. I didn't think that was so funny.

"Well, she couldn't have been *that* spry," I told the real estate agent. "She died, didn't she?"

The woman ignored me. She was a prissy, somewhat strict little lady in her forties, with a pointed face and her hair fashioned in tight little curls. The real estate lady had a double chin. Under the second chin was a necklace. Something was hanging from the bottom of the necklace. I looked to see if it was a cross, but it wasn't. It was some jeweled thing.

"Not only that," said the real estate lady, now addressing her comments to just my sister, "but Miss Elizabeta had just returned from an extensive sightseeing tour of China. Miss Elizabeta said she required just one pair of sensible shoes for the entire trip. She said the tour really tired her out, though. Actually, it was the last trip she took before she died. Oh, that Miss Elizabeta was sure a hoot." The real estate agent cackled again.

Nettie tried to laugh. Nettie's the nice Nettlestein.

"Maybe if Miss Elizabeta had taken more than one pair of shoes," I said, "she'd be alive today."

The real estate agent led my sister to another room. Nettie looked over her shoulder at me as she walked away, and gave me an angry look.

The more we got to know about Miss Elizabeta, the more

interesting the woman became, and the more we liked her and her home. Imagine, Miss Elizabeta had the same address and phone number and lived in the same house her entire life. How many people do you know never changed their phone number or address? Ever.

The real estate agent told us that during her long lifetime, Miss Elizabeta had ventured out of Bowling Green many times. She said Miss Elizabeta had gone to China, as she had mentioned, explored Alaska, traveled up the Amazon River, and studied French at the Sorbonne in Paris. Then Miss Elizabeta returned to Bowling Green to teach French at Western Kentucky University, which was a stone's throw away from her (soon-to-be our) front porch. The real estate agent had been one of her students. She said Miss Elizabeta was someone everybody in Bowling Green, Kentucky, knew, loved, and talked about.

What else, I wondered, did they have to talk about in Bowling Green, Kentucky? But I didn't say it.

I think the real estate lady pitied my sister. I'm sure she thought Nettie was doomed to endless years with her Hebrew husband. I'll bet she thought Nettie was Nordic.

7

We bought the house. The real estate lady threw in the glider on the front porch as part of the deal.

"Wasn't that nice of her?" said Nettie.

"It was easier than taking the damn thing down and making arrangements to cart it away," I muttered.

"That's ridiculous. You were angry with that real estate lady, weren't you? Why were you so angry with her, Jimmy?"

"I wasn't angry."

"Yes, you were. You were downright hostile to that woman. Why were you being so hostile to her?"

"That woman hates Jews."

"Who hates Jews?"

"The real estate agent. She hates Jews. Couldn't you tell? She spoke to you all the time because you don't look Jewish. I look Jewish, so she didn't say a thing to me."

"The real estate agent doesn't hate Jews. You've got to get rid of this thing you have that Southerners dislike Jews."

"Well, *that* woman hates Jews. I was telling her something and she just walked away, like I smelled bad or something."

"You *do* smell bad."

"I'll bet you money she's anti-Semitic."

"How much?"

"Five bucks," I said.

"Make it ten, Jimmy. No, make it twenty dollars."

"Okay, twenty bucks."

"The real estate agent doesn't hate Jews," said my sister. "She just hates you. The real estate agent's Jewish, for God's sake. Her name is Rachel Goldstein. Give me my twenty bucks."

8

Nettie and I had more furniture than we could use. Between Nettie's house and my apartment, every room of our house on Chestnut Avenue was overfurnished.

The two of us generally had breakfast out. But in the fall, when school started, Nettie began cooking breakfast at home. She had her lunch on campus and I'd grab a bite at Theresa's Restaurant. My sister usually cooked our dinners. Nettie took to Southern cooking as though she had been born and raised in Atlanta, Georgia. I started calling her Rhett until she told me Rhett was the guy.

After classes began at Western Kentucky University, Nettie and I had dinner at home a lot. One night Nettie said, "I think we ought to start saying grace before we eat."

"How do you do grace?"

"You bow your head, and clasp your hands together, and say a short prayer to thank God for all the blessings in our lives. You generally say grace at dinner, though I've seen some students saying grace at lunch in the cafeteria."

"We're Jewish, Nettie. Jews don't say grace."

"It doesn't matter what religion you are."

"You sure?"

"Yes I'm sure. Say grace, Jimmy."

"I don't think I know how."

"Goddamn it, Jimmy, say grace!"

"Thank you, God, for the pork chops. They really look good."

"That'll do, I suppose," said my sister, and we started eating.

After dinner I was rocking back and forth on our front porch in one of the rocking chairs we'd bought at Cracker Barrel. Nettie was in the kitchen stacking dishes into the dishwasher. I had finished my chores, which consisted of clearing the dinner table, emptying the garbage, and walking Hortense. I was relaxing, while the damn dog was snoozing on her chinchilla mat. Nettie'd bought half a dozen chinchilla mats for Hortense to lie down on, and scattered them around the house. I couldn't believe my sister did that. Now the damn dog wouldn't lay on anything that wasn't fur. Hortense *really* annoyed me. She was the only four-legged creature I knew who could push my buttons.

The campus was quiet during our first months in Bowling Green. Nettie busied herself setting up house and getting her teaching plans in order. She took over the den and made the room her office. I spent most of my time on one of our two rockers on the front porch. I'd rock the days away, reading a good book, sitting in front of an electric fan, a glass of sweet iced tea in my hand, enjoying myself. Most nights I did the same thing.

When Nettie finished with the dinner dishes and joined me, I wanted to make sure to tell her what a really great idea it was of hers to move to Bowling Green, Kentucky. Once you got used to the excruciatingly slow pace, the good manners, the blistering summer heat, and all the y'alls, Bowling Green was a truly fun town with really nice people.

Our house was a wonderful house, the sweet iced tea was

refreshing, Reilly's Bakery's "long john" pastries were scrumptious, and Bowling Green's Steak 'n Shake had the greatest hamburgers and milk shakes in the country. In fact, their shakes were *too* thick. Most times I couldn't get any of the shake up my straw. I hated that. Nettie loved it. Plus once I had stopped being a podiatrist I didn't have asthma anymore. Just like Nettie had said. I wanted to make sure to tell Nettie my feeling about our move South. It would make her feel good. Reinforce her thinking that she had made the right decision for both of us.

I never got the chance to bestow my many compliments on my sister. As soon as Nettie hit the porch she said, "Instead of rocking your life away, why don't you get off your lazy behind and go find yourself an office? Get to work. We could use the money."

9

In less than a week I found what I considered to be the perfect office.

The location was the center of town. The entrance to the outdoor stairway up to my floor was just across the street from the small town square. When you climbed the stairs to the first and only level, a travel agency was on one side of the landing, and my little detective agency would soon be on the other.

My sister had checked the Bowling Green Yellow Pages and decided that if I called my company anything that began with an *A*, I would be the first private detective agency listed in the directory. The front door of my office, the one with the yellow opaque glass, had painted on it:

AMERICA'S DETECTIVES, Inc.
Jimmy Netts—Chief Detective

My office consisted of two and a half rooms. The place came with some assorted furniture, stuff the previous tenant obviously didn't want and left behind. There was a reception room, a small hallway, and a bathroom and shower off the hall. My office was in the front of the building facing the Village Square.

On the day after Labor Day, a gloomy Tuesday in September, I opened my office for business. Tuesday just happened to be a *mazel-dickey* day.

(A *mazel-dickey* day means a lucky day.)

I was now officially a private eye.

I spent my first morning reading the newspaper, going out for coffee and drinking it at the coffee shop, then going out again and bringing the second cup back to have at my desk.

A little before noon I took my lunch break. I went to Theresa's Restaurant and sat at the counter. I made it a point to go to Theresa's because they had a great-looking waitress working there named Katie Canary. I never said anything to Katie, just ordered my lunch. I'm not very smooth. Ordering my lunch from Katie was enjoyable enough.

A month later I hired the Cheesy Secretary.

Her name was Mrs. Trixie Forenski.

Trixie was thirty-four years old. According to her, she was part Polish, part Romanian, part Croatian, and part Latvian. Trixie spent most of the morning putting on her eyeliner and mascara, and most of the afternoon doing her nails. Her fingernails looked like eagle's talons. She pasted American flags, and dragons, and sparkles, and little gold stars, and God knows what else on them. Trixie was dark and had a quasi-Italian look. In some ridiculous way, Trixie Forenski was pretty.

Trixie wore very short dresses. She was a big girl with big boobs and big thighs, and Trix didn't seem to want to cover up any of them. When she crossed her legs she showed lots of thigh. When she bent over to pick up a piece of paper or some trash, most of her bosom was visible. All of this would be quite pleasurable for the waiting room's male clientele, if there ever was a waiting room clientele.

One afternoon, after Trixie had gone to lunch, I got up and

walked to one of my windows. Both of my office windows overlooked the Village Square, which I thought should have been called the Village Rectangle because that's what it was. It was two blocks long and one block wide.

Anyway, looking out my window at the Village Rectangle, I thought how different things were in the South than in the North. In the South, Southerners talked differently. They said *mah* for my, *bah* for by. They spoke melodically, said y'all for you all. Southerners made all their *er*'s into *ah*'s. They said *fathah* instead of father and *mothah* instead of mother.

In the South they seemed to eat more than in the North. Southerners even joked about it. They said in Southern zoos there was a description of the animal on the front of its cage, along with a recipe. There was also a joke about how mannerly Southern ladies were. It was said that Southern women had such good manners they rarely participated in orgies. Too many thank-you notes.

Also Southerners paraded their crazy relatives around at every opportunity. The Southern grandfather who always did an embarrassing jig was dragged out of the attic at parties and told to do his dance. The great-auntie who constantly babbled, "Dabba dabba doo doo doo," was made to chatter like a fool at all family social gatherings. In the North it was entirely different. We hid the crazies. I had an aunt who peed in potted plants. We never asked her to do that for guests.

Someone cleared his throat. I whirled around and saw a well-dressed old man standing on the other side of my desk.

"Are you Mr. Netts?" he said.

"Yes, I am."

"Are you a private detective?"

"Yes, I am."

"I want you to find out who murdered my son."

SEVEN

JIMMY'S FIRST CASE

I

"Let me introduce myself. I am Arthur Deco Senior. My son, Arthur Deco Junior, was murdered in New York. Are you capable of finding out who murdered him? Yes or no."

"I most certainly am capable of finding who murdered your son, sir," I replied. I was amazed at how calm and confident I was for my first case, and a murder case at that. "What's your son's name?"

"I just told you. Arthur Deco Junior. Not a good sign, Mr. Netts."

I winced internally at my stupidity.

Arthur Deco Senior was tall and distinguished-looking. He appeared to be permanently angry. Not one to mess with or be impolite to. He had a full head of pure white hair parted in the center, a hawklike nose, and piercing eyes. His lips were thin and stiff, and he stood erect as a West Point cadet. The elderly man was wearing a starched white-collared shirt with a rep tie, and, even though it was summer, a well-made three-piece gray suit. He held a wooden cane under his arm like a crop. The cane had a silver grip.

"How long have you been a private detective?" he asked.

"Almost twenty years," I lied. "Nineteen in Philadelphia, and about a year here, roughly. How did you find me, Mr. Deco?"

"You were the first detective agency in the Yellow Pages."

Good old Nettie.

"So, Mr. Netts, what was your biggest case?"

"Two married couples, all four murdered by a serial killer," I said without missing a beat. "The killer made the four murders appear to look like suicides."

"Suicides, you say?" said Mr. Deco Senior, rubbing his chin with his left hand, leaning on the cane with his right. "Interesting. Carry on."

Carry on?

"The killer hung the bodies all over Philadelphia: one guy from a boathouse on the Schuylkill River, one girl from the Rocky statue in front of the Philadelphia Museum, one from—"

"This killer made all four deaths look like suicides?" interrupted Mr. Deco Senior. The suicide angle obviously intrigued him.

"Yes sir," I said, "the serial killer made all the murders appear to be suicides."

"Hmmm," he hmmmed.

Actually, the murders took place in a Peter Lovesey book I was reading called *The Secret Hangman*. The murders didn't take place in Philadelphia, Pennsylvania, but Bath, England. I hadn't finished the book yet, so I hoped the old man wouldn't ask me how I solved the murders.

"How did you solve the murders, Mr. Netts?" asked Mr. Deco Senior.

I looked around the room for someone called Netts, then remembered it was me. It had been over six months and I still hadn't gotten used to being called Netts and not Nettlestein. "Uh . . . it's a long story. Just chalk it up to good investigative work."

"How much do you charge?" he asked.

"Excuse me, sir?"

"I asked you, what do you charge?"

My going rate for murders was something I never talked to Nettie about.

"Uh . . . a hundred dollars a day and expenses?" I said. I forgot who charged a hundred dollars a day and expenses. It may have been Philip Marlowe. Or maybe it was Nick Charles.

"If you solve this case, Mr. Netts, I'll pay you a *thousand* dollars a day and expenses."

"A thou—"

"I'm a very wealthy man, Mr. Netts," said old man Deco. "I founded my own company, Deco Industries. Our home office is here in Bowling Green. If it wasn't for Deco Industries, half this town would be unemployed. We have seventy branch offices worldwide. My company is the one-hundred-and-third-largest company in America. At least that's what *Forbes* magazine says."

"You'll give me a thousand dollars a day?" I muttered, still in shock over the old man's announcement.

"Stay with me, Mr. Notts," snapped Deco. "I want—"

"Netts."

"Say what?"

"My name is Netts, not Notts."

"I don't like to be interrupted, Mr. Netts."

"But you said my name wrong. You called me Notts. My name is Netts. I think that's worth interrupting you."

"Also, Mr. Netts, I will neither be corrected, nor will I permit insolence."

I thought, If I want the thousand dollars a day, I better back off.

"Okay, Mr. Deco, I won't interrupt you or correct you ever again."

"Sit down, Mr. Netts," ordered Arthur Deco Senior.

I sat down. Senior was still standing, looming over me, leaning on his cane.

"Two weeks ago," said old man Deco, "my son Arthur Deco Junior was murdered in his Manhattan apartment."

"I'm sorry for your loss," I said.

"Yes . . . well . . . all right. He was shot and killed on July twelfth. On July fourteenth I was told by the New York Police Department my son committed suicide. I said that wasn't possible. I said my son didn't have the nerve to commit suicide. I said it takes guts to put a gun to your temple and pull the trigger. Someone murdered my son, then placed the murder weapon in his hand. I told that to the police too. Another thing, Mr. Netts. There wasn't a note. I understand most suicides leave notes. The police think that even though Junior didn't leave a note and didn't have a history of depression, he still killed himself. Well, they're full of baloney. My son didn't kill himself. My son was murdered. I'm *sure* of that, Mr. Netts. I'm absolutely *sure* of that."

"Isn't this a matter for the NYPD?"

"No!" shouted the furious old man. And then, calming down a bit, he said, "I just told you, the New York Police Department will not do anything more about my son's murder!" The old man inhaled deeply and went on. "The New York City Police Department keeps saying my son committed suicide. By saying that, the police can get rid of a big problem. Now they don't have to solve anything. My son's murder is not even on their precinct's books anymore. Do you understand what I'm saying, Mr. Netts?"

"Yes sir, I do."

"Good."

"Were someone else's fingerprints on the gun?" I asked, sensing the question was probably a dumb one.

"Of course not. The gun was wiped clean. How many murder cases have you had where the murderer's fingerprints were on the murder weapon when the police got there?"

"None," I said truthfully.

"That's another thing I won't abide, Mr. Netts. Stupid questions. The murderer obviously wore gloves," continued old man Deco. "There weren't any suspicious fingerprints anywhere in the apartment."

There was quiet for a moment, then Mr. Deco said, "One week after it happened, without any investigation whatsoever, the New York Police Department felt confident enough to call Junior's murder a suicide. Can you imagine?"

"And . . . and you want to open the case?"

"Of course I do. I want to open the case immediately. I'm convinced my son was murdered, Mr. Netts. My son was gay. Everyone knows gay men are cowards. *You* know that. One must be a man in the full sense of the word and not a sick queer to be able to take your own life, particularly when shooting yourself in the head or mouth. Ernest Hemingway had the balls to kill himself, pardon my French. He put that shotgun in his mouth and pulled the damned trigger with his toe. Hemingway was a man. My son was a queer. He could never have done that. Gay men don't shoot themselves, period."

I was appalled at Mr. Deco's attitude toward gays and the words he used, but I said nothing. I needed the work. I scribbled in my notebook: *Deco says son was gay and didn't have nerve to kill himself. Says gays don't shoot themselves. I don't care what Nettie says, this old fart hates Jews.*

Mr. Deco continued. "Two New York detectives who worked the case, a Lieutenant Edward Roach and a Detective Jacqueline Hallerhan in the Nineteenth Precinct, told me there was neither a note, nor was there a history of depression. Well, damn it, I could have told them that. Art was never depressed. That's another thing those police people do not realize. Faggots don't get depressed. Have you ever seen a depressed queer, Mr. Netts?"

I wrote the detectives' names in my notebook along with: *Faggots don't get depressed.*

"Did you go to New York?" I asked, sidestepping Mr. Deco's last question.

"What?"

"Did you go to New York to talk to the police? How did you find out the cops dropped the case a week later?"

"On the telephone, for God's sake."

Another stupid question.

"I see," I muttered.

There was some silence while I tried to think of a good question.

"Whose gun was it?"

"My son's, but so what?"

"Right. So what?" I wondered if becoming a private detective was such a good idea.

"Anyone could have gotten their hands on my son's gun," said Mr. Deco.

"Why's that?" I asked.

"Everyone knew where he kept it. Even I knew."

"Gotcha," I said knowingly.

"Again, let me repeat," said Arthur Deco Senior. "I told the two New York detectives over and over again my son was queer and that queers don't have the nerve to shoot themselves. I must have told them that a hundred times, but they *still* dropped the case."

Mr. Deco looked worn out.

"I want you to find out who killed Junior, Mr. Netts."

"I will, sir." And then I remembered a question detectives always asked on television. "Mr. Deco," I said, "did your son have any enemies, anyone who might have wanted to do him harm?"

Arthur Deco Senior was quick to answer. "Eddie Cotton."

"Who?"

"A lowlife named Eddie Cotton," said Mr. Deco. "My son's first . . . uh . . . er . . . boyfriend. I am certain this guy Cotton killed Junior. I despair that my son was murdered, but if that homo did it . . ."

Quiet filled my office.

"Eddie Cotton," I said.

"Yes, Eddie Cotton. This Cotton bozo used to be my son's . . . uh . . ."

"Partner," I said.

"Yes, partner, and this Cotton fellow had made some pretty bad threats against Junior since the two . . . uh . . . how should I put it?"

"Severed their relationship?"

"Yes. I am told some of those threats were extremely severe."

"Who told you about these threats?"

"Someone."

"And what did this 'someone' say Eddie Cotton said?"

"Threats . . . he made threats on my son's life."

"I'm sorry, Mr. Deco, to ask again, but can you tell me who made the threats and what the threats were?"

"I was told that threats were made," Senior said. "Let's let it go at that."

Mr. Arthur Deco Senior turned on his heel and walked out of my office.

2

That night at dinner I said to Nettie, "Before we start, I'd like to say grace."

"How nice. Go right ahead."

We bowed our heads and I said, "Thank you, dear God, for sending a client."

"I don't think that's what you say when you say grace."

"What the hell do you say?"

"You thank God for all of our blessings, and—"

"A client is a blessing if there ever was one, Nettie. Especially nowadays."

"Maybe so. But you *really* thank Him for the food that we are about to eat, for the love we have for each other. Those kinds of blessings."

"Is God a Him, Nettie?"

"Just eat, okay? So what's this about a new client?"

"Not only is this man my first client, but it's also my first murder case."

"What!" yelped Nettie, dropping her fork into her lap. "Tell me about it and don't leave out one single word."

"A man named Mr. Arthur Deco Senior dropped by the office and—"

"I've heard of him," said Nettie. "He's got buildings on campus with his name on them. The Arthur Deco, Sr., School of Business, The Arthur Deco, Sr., Mall."

"That's my new client, Nettie."

"Tell me about the case."

"Well," I said with relish and a mouthful of food, "it seems his son, Arthur De—"

"Chew," said Nettie. "It's revolting when you speak with food in your mouth. It looks like dirty clothes being tossed around in a dryer."

I chewed. And swallowed. "It seems," I said, "Arthur Deco Senior's son committed suicide in his apartment in New York two weeks ago."

"Oh, that's too bad," said Nettie. "How sad."

"Only old man Deco thinks his son was murdered. He thinks whoever killed him tried to make it *look* like a suicide. At least that's what Mr. Deco thinks. By the way, the NYPD say Arthur Deco Junior—that's the son's name, the son's Junior, the father's Senior—the NYPD say the son killed himself. They say it was suicide and not murder, and closed the case a week later. I think that's a short time, Nettie, don't you?"

"I have no idea."

"Mr. Deco's convinced his son was murdered. He said his son wouldn't have the nerve to kill himself because his son's gay."

"Gay people have the nerve to kill themselves."

"I know that, Nettie. Old man Deco is a homophobe."

"He is?" said Nettie. "That's a shame. He does so many good things for so many people."

"Anyway, I didn't want to say anything nasty to Deco and lose the case. I mean, I want to collect some salary and expense money. We can use it."

"We sure can. Will Mr. Deco pay you even if you *don't* solve this case?"

"I don't know. You and I never talked about that, or my fees and expenses. So when the old man asked me what I charged for murder, I started winging it. I told him a hundred dollars a day plus expenses. I think that's what Philip Marlowe, the private eye in Chandler's books, charged."

"Chandler wrote the Philip Marlowe books a thousand years ago."

"I didn't think of that."

I chewed my lip, disgusted with myself.

"That's okay," said Nettie.

"Mr. Deco said, 'If you solve this case I'll pay you *a thousand dollars* a day plus expenses!'"

"I suspect that's about what private eyes get these days. But that's terrific, Jimmy."

"I guess I don't get paid if I don't solve the case, Nettie. Old man Deco said, *'If you solve this case,* I'll pay you a thousand dollars' . . . et cetera."

"I guess you don't. That's stuff we need to remember for your next client. And Jimmy . . ."

"What?"

"Make sure to keep a list of your expenses."

"Okay."

There was a major pause in the conversation.

Then Nettie said, "I wonder why Mr. Deco thinks someone murdered his son and why he doesn't think his son committed suicide."

"Because suicides usually leave a note and his son didn't leave one. *And* his son wasn't depressed. Oh, and wait a minute." I checked my notes. "The old man said, 'That's because my son's a faggot and faggots don't have the—'"

"I hate the word faggot," said Nettie.

"I do too, Nettie, but that's the word the old man used. It's right there in my notes. He said because his son was a fagg—was gay, he didn't have the nerve to shoot himself. Obviously old man Deco hated his son for being a homosexual."

Nettie went, "Hummm," which usually meant something. Then she said, "Did Mr. Deco say anything else?"

"Yes. He said NYPD detectives called the case a suicide because they wanted to get it off the precinct's books. I think that's about it. Oh . . . and he told me to check out a guy named Eddie Cotton."

"Why?" asked my sister.

"Mr. Deco said that Eddie Cotton was Junior's former lover."

"Former lovers make good suspects," said Nettie.

"Now someone has replaced Cotton as the son's new lover."

"Replaced lovers make even better suspects than former lovers," said my sister.

"What're your thoughts about my next step, Nettie?"

"I'd call one of the detectives who worked the case in New York to make sure they'll be there. Then fly up and talk to the two detectives Mr. Deco mentioned. You have their names, right? Then, when you get all the information you can from the detectives, talk to this Cotton guy. Then come home and meet with the Deco family."

"Meet with the Deco family? Why?"

"Some of the Decos are homophobes. The ones that could be suspects," said Nettie.

EIGHT

THE NINETEENTH PRECINCT

I

The Nineteenth Precinct was located on Sixty-seventh Street between Lexington and Third Avenues. There was a firehouse next to the precinct, and a school somewhere on the block. A lot of school buses were lined up along the curb when I got to the corner.

I walked up the steps of the Nineteenth, pulled open a door, and went inside. On the walls inside the precinct were MOST WANTED posters, plaques, and an honor roll of Nineteenth Precinct cops who had distinguished themselves that month. On another wall were the police from the Nineteenth who were killed on September 11, 2001.

I would bet nothing had changed regarding the looks of things inside the Nineteenth Precinct since the 1800s. Just the uniforms. I went to the reception desk, a big curved thing with an oak top. There were several cops standing behind the desk.

"What can I do for you?" asked a husky lady sergeant.

"I'm . . . uh . . . I'm looking for the detectives who worked on the Deco murder . . . or rather the Deco suicide. I'm a private investigator from Bowling Green, Kentucky. I'm representing the murdered . . . the dead boy's father."

"Do you have any credentials?" asked the husky lady sergeant.

"No, but I have my business card," which I showed the police-woman.

"No credentials, huh?"

"They don't issue credentials to private investigators in Kentucky," I explained. "You just use your business card."

"You have no credentials, right?" repeated the lady cop.

"I've come all the way from Bowling Green, Kentucky, ma'am. I really would appreciate—"

"Hold on, buster." The husky woman cop walked away from the counter.

Buster?

Fifteen minutes later a much cuter lady cop, not in a uniform, dressed in a pants suit, came out from behind a pair of swinging doors. She spoke to the husky lady sergeant at the desk, who pointed to me sitting on a bench along a wall. The lady cop in the pants suit made her way toward me. I stood up.

"Hello. I'm Detective Hallerhan," she said. "What can I do for you?" She extended her hand to shake. I shook it.

I explained who I was and who I represented.

"You have any credentials?" she asked.

"No, but I have a—"

"Business card. Yeah. I know."

"They don't have credentials for PIs in Kentucky."

"So you say. Why did Mr. Deco hire a private investigator?" asked Detective Hallerhan.

"Because I don't think he trusts the New York Police Department. That's from him, not me. He's told me over and over how he's thought all along that his son was murdered, but that you guys classified his death as a suicide."

"We, my partner and me, we *never* thought the vic was a suicide," said Hallerhan, bristling with anger, "never conclusively. I can't say more than that."

"Hey, I'm only telling you what the . . . what the vic's father told me," I said, getting a kick out of using the word vic. "This isn't me speaking."

"Sorry for jumping on you," said the detective, "but my partner and I are really goosey about this one. We wanted to stay on the case. We're still touchy about it, as you can see. Maybe the ME's full report will change things, or the—"

"What can the ME's report tell you?" I knew that an ME was the medical examiner, from all the detective programs and movies I've watched.

"Maybe something that might suggest murder so we could open the case again."

"And the ballistics report?"

"If they dug a different bullet out of the wall than the one fired from the vic's suicide gun, then it means another gun was used to shoot the victim, and we'd have an honest-to-goodness murder on our hands. But we're not getting our hopes up about that because it's a long shot. Anyway, that's what the ballistics report could tell us."

"I see. Detective Hallerhan, may I ask you a few more questions about the Deco case?"

Hallerhan told me to follow her. She led me back through the swinging doors, around a corner, and eventually to a large room with a bunch of desks in it. She took me to her desk, pointed to a chair beside it, and asked me to please sit down. Across from her was a kind of nice-looking older detective. I could tell he was a detective because he didn't wear a uniform, and he had a large black gun holstered to his belt. His suit coat hung from the back of his desk chair.

"Lieutenant?" said Hallerhan, speaking to the cop sitting across from her. "This guy says he's a PI representing Arthur Deco Junior's father and wants to ask me some questions about the case."

The detective pushed back his desk chair and, using his feet, walked the chair around so that he ended up sitting beside me in the aisle.

"My name's Lieutenant Eddie Roach," he said to me, extending his hand. "Detective Hallerhan caught the Deco case. I was just supervising it. And you are . . ."

I shook his hand and said, "I'm—"

"Like I said, this guy says he represents Deco's father," repeated Hallerhan. "He doesn't have any credentials, just a business card. He could be any *schlump,* someone from the newspapers, who knows?"

(*Schlump* means a dull or slovenly person.)

I decided, right then and there, to tell the detectives the truth.

"Okay, Officers, I'm going to come as clean as a whistle. I'm an *unlicensed* private detective from Bowling Green, Kentucky. I've just opened an office there. I've never been a private detective before in my entire life. And again, I am *not* licensed. I've never had a license. I was a half-ass podiatrist in Philadelphia. My sister talked me into moving with her to Kentucky. My sister, Nettie Nettlestein, is a professor of art history at Western Kentucky University. Western Kentucky's in Bowling Green. Western's got a great basketball team. They're called the Hilltoppers.

"Anyway, my sister said being a podiatrist gave me asthma and once I quit I wouldn't have asthma anymore. Nettie, that's my sister's name, Nettie was absolutely right about that. My asthma's gone since I stopped examining feet. Nettie persuaded me to move from Philly to Bowling Green with her. The main reason I moved to Bowling Green with Nettie was because she said in Bowling Green I could be anything I wanted to be.

"So I decided to become a private detective. Truth be told, what I've always *really* wanted to be was a detective, like you guys. I've read every mystery and police procedural I could get my hands on. And I've seen every whodunit movie that's ever been made. I guess private investigator is as close as I'll come to being a detective."

The two detectives were listening to me, as if what I was saying were really interesting. So I continued.

"As I said, I'm an *unlicensed* private detective. I made up all that stuff about in Kentucky PIs only have business cards. I'm sure they have licenses. The only case I've had since I opened my office is this one. A murder case! Would you believe it? I've got to admit it, Officers, I'm flying by the seat of my pants. Murder is way out of my bailiwick. When it comes to detective work, I haven't a clue what's *in* my bailiwick.

"I can tell you two this. Old man Deco is a really ornery son-of-a-bitch. I don't know if it's such a blessing having him as a client. He found me because I'm the first name in the Bowling Green Yellow Pages. I'm listed as America's Detectives, Inc. That was my sister's idea, making my company start with an *A* in the Yellow Pages. It was a great idea. It put me at the top of the list. If she hadn't done that, I wouldn't be here today. But then, I don't know if it's such a good thing that I'm here today.

"Anyway, Deco said he would pay me a thousand dollars a day plus expenses if I could prove his son was murdered and didn't commit suicide. He told me to start with a guy named Eddie Cotton, and I—"

"He said Eddie Cotton murdered his son?" said Hallerhan.

"No, he didn't say that, Detective Hallerhan. Deco said he *thought* this guy Cotton murdered his son. I asked him why he figured Cotton to be the killer, and he said . . ." I pulled out my trusty notebook. "He said: '*This Cotton fellow has made some pretty bad threats against Junior in the past, I'm told.*' And when I asked old man Deco who told him about these threats Cotton allegedly made against his son, he said: '*I was told that threats were made. Let's let it go at that.*'" I shut my notebook. "Then the old buzzard walked out of my office. That's everything I know. Like I said, I don't have a lick of experience. None whatsoever. I'm *really* flying by the seat of my pants."

I slumped back in my chair, exhausted.

"We'll help you," said Detective Eddie Roach. "We'll tell you what we know."

2

The two detectives explained all the pertinent facts of the Deco suicide/murder to me. I listened attentively, and made notes.

They told me about the body being found on the floor of Deco's apartment. They explained how the murder (the two were convinced it was murder) was made to look like a suicide, and how the weapon, a Beretta 9mm automatic, was lying on the rug in Art Deco's right hand. They said the gun was registered under Deco's name, that a bullet—the one that went through Deco's head—was buried in a nearby wall. The two took turns telling me the bullet was removed from that wall and sent to ballistics, that the casing on the floor was "probably" the same casing used in the murder/suicide gun in Deco's hand, and that the bullet in the wall "most likely" would be the same bullet fired from that gun, though the ballistics report hadn't come back from the lab yet. And neither had the medical examiner's report.

"Both reports are taking forever to get to us," said Detective Hallerhan.

They told me how, according to Deco's roommate, a guy named Tim Duncan, Deco hadn't left a note, which most suicides usually do; was rarely depressed, which most suicides usually are; and that Deco was left-handed.

"If Deco really was left-handed," said the lieutenant to me, "why was the gun in his *right* hand? Left-handed people don't usually shoot themselves with their right hand. *And* if Deco really shot himself, why was the gun still in his hand after he fell to the floor? My bones keep telling me, and have been all along, this one's murder."

Roach told me his boss and precinct commander, Captain Joseph Bigatel, *suggested* the case be changed to a suicide and dropped, and Lieutenant Roach concurred.

"Why did you concur, Lieutenant? Didn't you just say your bones told you Deco was murdered?"

"Yeah, my bones smelled murder," said the lieutenant, "but I generally accept what the captain *suggests* I should accept. It's good politics."

"Your boss ruled kind of quickly, didn't he?" I asked.

"Yeah, he did," said Detective Hallerhan sullenly. "A week later. We dropped the case before we interviewed any wits."

"Wits?" I asked.

"Witnesses. Hey, do us a favor," said Hallerhan. "Don't go to Captain Bigatel to discuss this case, okay? This case is officially closed."

"I won't. I promise. So way down deep, you guys think Deco Junior was murdered, right?"

"Yeah, but like Jackie says, that's just between us," said Eddie Roach. "Like I just told you, when the boss says it's suicide, and I go on record agreeing with him, it's over. We don't keep hammering away on a case we're not allowed to touch. We've got to drop it and move on, unless . . ."

"Unless what?" I asked.

"Unless you find something *really* unusual," said Lieutenant Roach.

"If the case had gone on, you know, hadn't been shut down," I asked, "who would your main suspects have been?"

Lieutenant Roach took a deep breath and let it out. "I'd agree with the vic's father. I'd say the ex-boyfriend, Eddie Cotton, would be our number one suspect. He was the jilted lover. That's one. I'd also include the father. We were told he was a big-time homophobe. He might have killed his son because he was gay. Stranger things have been known to happen. The father wasn't around his son's apartment building the day his kid was murdered. At least nobody saw him come or go. But that doesn't mean he couldn't have gained access to his son's apartment some other way. Like going up in the service elevator. That's two suspects. The vic's sister was definitely in and out of the victim's apartment. She's supposedly a world-class homophobe like her father. That's three. We'd talk to the new lover too."

"Who, Duncan?" I asked.

"Yeah, Duncan. They may have had an argument. Who knows? That's four. Maybe after investigating the case we'd find one or two more. But Cotton would have been high on our list."

As I got up to leave, Detective Hallerhan said, "I'm sorry I called you a *schlump*."

3

The next day I grabbed a cab and went out to Flushing to question Eddie Cotton. Lieutenant Roach had given me Cotton's address. He told me to keep him and Detective Hallerhan informed of everything I found out. All of a sudden I felt like I was doing detective things. It felt good.

Flushing, New York, was street after street of row houses with iron bars on the front doors and first-floor windows. Just about every house had a three-step stoop leading to the front door. I'd thought Flushing was predominantly Italian, but I saw lots of Chinese and Korean restaurants and grocery stores.

I guess I'd been wrong about it being Italian.

It was a warm July morning when I walked up the three-step stoop at 140–35 Robinson Street and rang the doorbell. And oldish woman came to the door, opened it, and stood staring at me as if I were R2-D2.

"Does a Mr. Cotton live here?" I asked.

"Who?" asked the woman. She was wearing a thin bathrobe over a long light dress.

"Mr. Cotton."

"You have the wrong house," said the woman, pulling the neck of her robe tighter. She started to close the door.

"Does someone named Eddie live here?"

"Yeah, my son Eddie. Eddie Cantelone."

"Can I please speak to him?" I said, showing Mrs. Cantelone my buzzer, against my sister's wishes.

(A *buzzer* is slang for a police badge. At least it was in the old Dashiell Hammett detective books. I bought the badge at a police supply store.)

"Oh my God! Are you police?"

"Well, not exact—"

"Oh, my God," repeated Mrs. Cantelone. I thought she might faint.

I should have listened to Nettie. She said, "Under no circumstances are you to flash your buzzer."

Five minutes later, a bleary-eyed Eddie Cantelone, aka Eddie Cotton, came to the door. He stood there staring at me. Cotton was one of those guys I couldn't stand on sight. He wore a wife-beater underwear shirt, long dark blue track pants with a white stripe down the sides, no socks, and sandals. He had a thick, black head of hair, a very black five o'clock shadow, a cocky smirk, and bushels of hair growing under his armpits.

"Who the fuck are you?" was the way Eddie Cotton greeted me.

"I'm Jimmy Netts. I'm a private detective."

"A private dickey? An honest-to-goodness private dickey? Yeah? So whattaya gonna be dickin' me about, private dickey?"

All his "dickey" stuff amused the hell out of Cotton. He laughed hysterically at his clever (he thought) repartee.

"I want to talk to you about the Deco murder."

The *putz* stopped laughing.

(A *putz* is a jerk.)

"Don't you mean the Deco *suicide*?" he said.

"No. I mean the Deco *murder*."

"They change it from suicide to murder?"

"Yeah," I lied.

"So *you* say."

"Yeah, so I say."

"This should be good. So whattaya wanna ask me, dude?"

"May I come in . . . dude?"

"Yeah."

The small Cantelone living room was filled with too many sofas, armchairs, and ottomans. And every piece of furniture was covered with a plastic see-through slipcover. I never saw so much plastic in my life. There was a statue of Jesus on the cross standing on the fireplace mantel. The fireplace's hearth had fake logs in it.

Eddie Cantelone sat down in the biggest, most comfortable chair in the living room. He put his feet up on the armchair's matching ottoman and said, "So whattaya want?"

"May I sit down?"

"Yeah. Sit."

"Thank you," I said. I *really* didn't like this guy. "I'd like to ask you a few questions if I may, Mr—"

But before I could, Eddie's mother came into the living room and sat down beside me on a small settee.

"Mama, leave us alone. Please, go in the kitchen and let the man and me talk privately."

"What have you done, Eddie?" asked a very worried Mrs. Cantelone.

"Nothin', Mama. This guy's not a cop. He's just some half-ass investigator, an' I'm gonna try and help him out, okay? So please stay in the kitchen and let us talk privately. Okay?"

"What's he investigatin', Eddie?"

"Nothin' that means anythin' to you," said Eddie Cotton.

Mrs. Cantelone stood and left the room.

"I've already mentioned that Deco's suicide has been changed to murder," I said, "and you, Mr. Cotton, are one of the prime suspects."

"Who says?"

"The cops say."

"Well, they're fuckin' right."

"They *are*."

"About it being a murder. Art Deco could no more blow his brains out than I could. If it really was murder, then yeah, sure, I'd be a prime suspect. I was the rejected lover, wasn't I? I was thrown outta the apartment, wasn't I? I was left penniless *and* homeless. Yeah, sure, I *ought* to be the prime suspect."

"Art Deco's father is convinced *you* did it."

"He is, is he? Well, Art Deco's father can take that fuckin' thought and stick it up his—"

"Does anyone want coffee?" asked Mrs. Cantelone, sneaking back into the living room.

"No, Mama," said an irritated Eddie Cantelone. "*Please,* Mama. Stay in the kitchen and let us talk."

I gave Mrs. Cantelone time to leave the room, then asked, "Do you think Art Deco committed suicide?"

"I just told you, no way. He didn't have the guts."

"Was Art Deco ever depressed, Mr. Cotton?"

"Never. Maybe just a little now and then, but don't we all get depressed a little now and then? But I'll tell you this, Art was never depressed enough to put a bullet through his head. Even if he was that depressed, he wouldn't have the *cojones* to do that."

(*Cojones* means testicles.)

184

"Mr. Cotton, do you know anyone else who might have wanted to kill your former . . . uh . . . roommate?"

Eddie Cotton got up and walked out of the living room. I waited, wondering where the hell he went.

When he came back he said, "Just checkin' on my mom. I wanted to make sure she was in the kitchen. Don't want her, or my dad, overhearin' that I'm gay. They'd have a shit fit. An don't be callin' me Cotton around my mother and father. I'm Cantelone around here. Anyways, you were talkin' about my *roommate*? That's a nice way of puttin' it, ain't it? Roommate. Try lover. You asked who wanted to kill him? Plenty a people wanted to kill him."

"Like who?"

"Besides me? Try some members of Art's family. They have some rotten gay-bashers in that family. Particularly the father and one of the sisters. The sister named Hattie. The father and the sister wanted to kill the little prick maybe even more than I did. They hated the thought that a queer was in the great Deco family. I'm tellin' ya, if his father didn't kill him, his sister did."

"Which sister?"

"I just told ya. You ain't listenin' to me, private dickeyman. The one named Hattie. Art always told me his father and his sister Hattie hated gays. Some of the things those two said about gays were . . . were . . ."

Cotton was shaking his head, lost for words. I didn't pursue it.

"Anyways," he said, "the others in Art's family were okay with the gay thing. At least that's what Art said. But not the father and that one sister."

"Did you ever meet any of Deco's family?"

"No. I avoided his family and Art avoided mine. Anyway, good riddance, I say."

"Good riddance to who? Art's family?"

"No. To Art, the fuckhead," said Cotton angrily.

"Deco threw you over for another guy, right?"

"Yeah. So what?" said Cotton, bristling.

"They say there's nothing like a spurned lover for a good murder suspect."

"That's what they say, is it?" said Eddie Cotton. "Listen, Mr. Private Dickeyhead, I *wanted* to kill the little bastard in the worst way. I went to his apartment plannin' on stranglin' the scumbag with my own hands. That's what I was gonna do, I swear. I wanted to kill him in the worst way. For one thing, he had just reneged on a huge financial promise to me in a very sneaky way. For a second thing, the son-of-a-bitch ran off with another guy and left me standin' at Teterboro Airport twiddlin' my goddamn thumbs, worried to death about him. For a third thing, the bastard threw me out on the street without a cent to my name too. Three pretty good reasons to kill the little fucker, don'tcha think?"

"So did you kill Art Deco Junior?"

"No. Unfortunately, the bastard was dead when I got there."

4

Before I left New York I spent the morning at Arthur Deco Junior's apartment building. I spoke to the concierge, Michael Saffeiodi, and asked if I could look around the building.

"You another cop or somethin'?"

"Yes, working out of the Nineteen." I flashed the concierge my buzzer. Sort of now you see it, now you don't. "Can I see the vic's apartment? Oh, and is there a back entrance?"

"Yeah," said the concierge. "I'll get one a the guys to take you up and show to the late Mr. Deco's pad. Hey, Gelso. Come here a minute."

An apartment building employee whose name—GELSO—was stitched over his left blue denim work shirt pocket, came to the front desk.

"Take this cop up to Deco's apartment," ordered the concierge. "Take him up by the service elevator, and down by the regular elevators."

I thanked the concierge and walked off with Gelso.

5

Back in Bowling Green I spent my entire first day and evening on the front porch of our house rocking and thinking about the murder/suicide. I was beginning to agree with Roach and Hallerhan. Art Deco Junior was murdered. But who did it?

"Dinner's ready!" hollered Nettie from the dining room.

"I'm not hungry, Nettie."

"Well, come and keep me company."

When I arrived at the dinner table, Nettie told me I had to eat *something*. So I grudgingly ate a couple of pork chops, some applesauce, two potato pancakes, some green beans, and a small piece of peach pie. And then another small piece of peach pie.

"So what do you think?" Nettie asked.

"I'm confused, Nettie. I don't know what to think. To tell you the truth, I'm sorry I became a private eye."

"Good Lord," she said, shaking her head, and went back to eating her dinner with the biggest, saddest eyes I ever saw.

Nettie was upset.

"Aw, don't you worry, Nettie, I'll figure something out." And then I told her about my conversation with Cotton. "I mean, it's a big responsibility, finding and convicting a killer. Anyway, I'm convinced the *mummzer* killed Art Deco."

"I didn't know you knew that word," said my sister.

"What word?"

"Mummzer."

"What's it mean?" I asked.

"It means rotten rat fink bastard. And who's the *mummzer*?"

"Cotton's the *mummzer,* and he did it. The *mummzer* said Art was already dead when he got to Deco's apartment, but I don't believe him."

"The *mummzer* seems like the obvious murderer to me too," my sister said agreeably. "He's the scorned lover, right? The one who was put out on the street when his boyfriend got himself a *new* boyfriend. The *mummzer* didn't deserve to be thrown out on the street. And penniless, to boot. He didn't do anything to warrant that kind of punishment and Deco could have set him up financially for six months or so until Cotton got himself back on his feet. All of that adds up to this guy Cotton having the perfect reason to kill Mr. Deco's son. Even the victim's father thinks he's the one. But in all the mysteries you've made me read, and in all the mystery movies and TV shows we watched, it was never the *obvious* one who committed the murder."

"I almost believe the bastard," I said.

"Which bastard?" asked Nettie. "Are you talking about the *mummzer*?"

"No. Old man Deco. He said he thought Cotton killed his son."

"Did you hear what I just said?"

"Yes, I heard you, Nettie. You said it's usually not the obvious one who's the murderer."

"I think you should go talk to the Deco family."

NINE

THE DECOS, AGAIN

I

I drove up a super-long driveway between white picket fences that led to the Deco mansion. There were rows of beech and maple trees on both sides of the road. About a dozen horses grazed behind the fences. The driveway was as wide as the street I had just driven off of, and almost as long. I presumed it led to the mansion and not to Nashville. Eventually a circular drive appeared that placed me and my car somewhere in the vicinity of the home's main entrance.

I had asked the entire Deco family to be present to answer some questions. Apparently they all came. Either that or Mr. and Mrs. Deco owned a lot of automobiles.

I was ushered into the living room by a butler who didn't say a word to me. All he did was usher me into the living room. Senior greeted me with a handshake. He was scowling when he said, "Mr. Netts." Not the cheeriest greeting I've ever received from a client. But then, I didn't have a hell of a lot of clients to compare him to.

Mrs. Margaret Deco, Senior's wife, stood and said to me, "So good of you to come." Under the circumstances, that seemed like an incredibly strange thing to say.

"I'm Mrs. Hattie Strange," said an angry-looking woman who neither stood nor bothered to look at me.

Miss Seena Deco, the twenty-two-year-old baby of the family, stood up, smiled sweetly, and said, "Nice to meet you, Mr. Netts."

I, of course, said, "Call me Jimmy."

And she, of course, didn't. It didn't matter. I fell in love again. Now I had two crushes in Bowling Green: Katie Canary the waitress and Seena Deco the heiress. Unfortunately, neither of the two ladies knew I was alive.

"And this is our other married daughter," said Mrs. Deco, nodding to a forlorn-looking young woman sitting at the far end of the large living room, "Mrs. Elizabeth Brown."

Mrs. Brown was a dumpy woman with a very plain face.

I walked up to her and said, "Hello, Mrs. Elizabeth Brown."

She stood and said, "You can call me Lizzie," looking down at her shoes.

"Okay, Lizzie. I'm Jimmy Netts. You can call me Jimmy."

Mrs. Brown nodded, said nothing, and sat down, her eyes never leaving her shoes.

"I am Barnsworth Bosley," said Barnsworth Bosley, a fat, neatly dressed man. He wore a tight-fitting black pin-striped suit he could barely get into, with a fly he couldn't quite close. It was obvious Bosley was another one of Senior's lawyers, perhaps his Bowling Green lawyer. "I am Mr. Deco's lawyer," said Bosley, "and this is my daughter, also a lawyer with our firm, Miss Erica Bosley. Miss Bosley is Mrs. Strange's lawyer."

Erica Bosley was in her early thirties, I'd guess, and skinny. She would have had a great body if she had an ass and tits. She was a mean-looking woman with bitch written all over her face. She wore a black dress and pearls. She was a head taller than I was, and could easily have passed for a man if she had to. Erica Bosley nodded hello with her eyes closed.

I sat down on a small couch.

"What do you want, Mr. Netts?" asked Hattie Strange, hardly a moment after I was seated.

"Well, Hattie—"

"Mrs. Strange to you."

"Absolutely . . . *Mrs.* Strange. You, and the others in this room, may or may not be aware of this, but your father hired me, at a thousand dollars a day, to find the murderer of *your* brother, and your parents' son."

That bit of news caused a great deal of a *rutabaga-rutabaga*.

(*Rutabaga-rutabaga* means a general muttering of voices around a room.)

I paused to let what I had just said sink in, proud of myself for being able to think of saying it. "I just have some questions I'd like to ask you."

"Like what?" asked Mrs. Hattie Strange, pushing me.

"I need more information," I said. "Like . . . is . . . is your son, and brother, I mean . . . *was* your son and brother right-handed or left-handed?"

"What difference does that make?" snorted old man Deco. "I can't see why that would have the slightest consequences with regard to my son's murder."

"Left-handed," said Seena. "The only one in the family who was."

"So, Mr. Netts, answer me," insisted the mean old bastard. "What difference does it make if my son was left- or right-handed?"

"Well, sir, the gun was lying on the floor in your son's *right* hand. If he was left-handed, as Seena . . . as Miss Deco—"

"You can call me Seena," she said.

"As Seena said he was, wouldn't your son normally shoot himself

195

with his *left* hand? So why was the gun in your son's *right* hand? That's a sort of difference, isn't it?"

More *rutabaga-rutabaga*.

Senior cleared his throat and said, "That *is* a good point, Mr. Netts. Exactly why I hired you. To find out information like that. The more evidence that proves my son was murdered, the better, I say. My son didn't commit suicide. He was murdered."

"Right now," I said, "the death of your son, Mr. and Mrs. Deco, has been classified as a suici—"

"Who did the classifying?" said Senior.

"The New York Police Department," I said.

"The New York Police Department's classifications aren't worth dog piddle," said Senior. "My son was murdered."

"Why are you so sure of that, Mr. Deco?"

"Because it takes guts to kill yourself and my son was gutless. I'm sorry to say that, but he was. Junior could no more shoot himself than I could . . . could . . . swim the Atlantic Ocean."

"Father, that was an awful thing to say," said Seena Deco.

"What was?"

"That Junior was gutless."

"Just stay out of this," said Senior to his daughter.

"Let me ask you all this question," I said. "Was young Arthur—"

"Call him Junior," ordered Mr. Deco. "Makes it easier. He's Junior. I'm Senior."

"Okay, to your knowledge, was . . . Junior . . . suffering from depression?"

Seena Deco said, "Absolutely not."

Mrs. Deco said, "Never. Not at all. Arthur is . . . was . . . always a happy child."

Lizzie said nothing. She just sat in her armchair, far away from the others, shoulders shrugged and scowling.

"Your son was living with another man," I said. "Was the family aware of that?"

Everyone but Lizzie murmured yes. She just shrugged her shoulders, as if to say it didn't matter to her whether her brother lived with someone or not.

"Does it matter to anyone in this room that Art was gay?" I asked.

"I object to that question," said lawyer Bosley. Nobody seemed to pay attention to him.

Seena Deco said, "It never mattered to me."

Arthur Deco Senior said, "Let's drop that subject."

"Why?" I asked.

"I said drop it," said Senior forcefully.

"Okay," I said. "I have other questions. Let's start with you . . . uh . . . Mr. Deco."

"Fine," he said.

"Did you go into your son's apartment building the day he was murdered?"

"I did *not*."

"And Mrs. Strange, did *you* go into your brother's apartment building the day he was murdered?"

"I object to that question," said Erica Bosley.

"Be quiet, Erica," said Hattie Strange. "I'll answer whatever questions I want to."

Erica Bosley slumped back in her armchair and frowned.

"Yes, Mr. Netts, I *did* visit my brother's apartment the afternoon he was found dead."

Mrs. Margaret Deco murmured something I couldn't hear. Senior appeared nonplussed.

"About what time was that, Mrs. Strange?"

"Sometime in the late afternoon. I'm not sure exactly when."

"Guess."

"Fourish."

"Did you go to your brother's apartment?"

"Yes," she answered.

"Why?"

"To kill him."

"My God, Hattie!" said Mrs. Deco.

"Hattie, be quiet, for God's sake," said Erica Bosley.

"You be quiet, Erica," snapped Mrs. Strange.

"Were you carrying a weapon?"

"Yes, I was. I had my husband's revolver in my purse."

Mrs. Deco looked as though she might faint.

"Are you all right, Mother?" asked her husband.

"Yes," she answered softly.

"Now I must insist—" began Barnsworth Bosley.

"How did you expect to get your husband's gun through airport security, Mrs. Strange?"

"I flew to New York with my father in his plane, Mr. Netts. There aren't any security problems when you have your own plane. Security doesn't check anything. Daddy owns his plane. It's a G4."

"Why did you want to kill your brother?"

"My brother was a diseased queer, and I was mortified. I was also frightened."

"Frightened? Of what?"

"That someone in my family might catch something."

"Catch what?"

"*Something*. Gay people all have *something* other people can catch. They're all sickos! They have AIDS, and lupus, and hepatitis, and—"

"And chicken pox, and mumps, and edema," Seena said.

"Are you making fun of me, Seena?"

"Yes, Hattie, I am."

"Well, I don't like being made fun of."

"I don't really care what you like or don't like, Hattie."

"Daddy?" whined Mrs. Strange.

Arthur Deco Senior said nothing.

"Did you use your husband's revolver to murder your brother?" I asked.

"Don't answer!" shouted the two Bosleys.

"No," said Hattie Deco Strange. "Someone beat me to it. By the time I got to my brother's apartment, he was already dead."

"Did you report it?"

"I did not."

"Why not?"

"For the umpteenth time, Mr. Netts, I was carrying a gun in my purse."

2

A week later Nettie and I were watching an old *Homicide* DVD in our living room.

"Jimmy."

"Yes?"

"Why don't you ask someone out and stop sitting around here every night?"

"Do I bother you?"

"Not at all. It's just that—"

"I thought we don't talk about affairs of the heart, Nettie. Anyway, who am I going to ask out?"

"Seena Deco," said Nettie.

"You must be kidding."

"The waitress at Theresa's, what's her name?"

"Katie Canary."

"Yes," said Nettie. "Call Katie."

"I'm outta practice, Nettie. I wouldn't know how to carry on a decent conversation with a woman for more than a minute and a half. I wouldn't even want to."

"You gotta get back up on that horse sometime, Jimmy."

"I don't see you getting back up on a horse."

We returned to watching television in silence.

On that particular episode of *Homicide*, a detective looked into a couple of cold case files, old cases that hadn't been solved, and found a clue to the murder he was working on. I went to the telephone.

"What do you want, Jimmy?" asked Lieutenant Eddie Roach in New York.

"You have any cold cases on your books, people killed at the time of Junior's death?"

"That's a strange question. Why do you ask?" he said.

"I was just watching one of those cop shows on television, *Homicide*, and one of the cops went to some old cold cases and somehow or other it helped the cop solve the murder case he was working on. At least it's an idea. I'm kind of lost, Eddie, and I can use any help I can get."

"Let me call you back," said Roach. "I'm in the middle of something right now."

I didn't think I'd hear from the lieutenant again, but twenty minutes later he called back and said, "We have lots of cold cases, but only three recent ones. One guy was shot in a tenement hallway."

"When was that?" I asked.

"Last January."

"That's too long ago, Eddie."

"One guy was found dead from stab wounds in an alley last March."

"Nothing more recent?"

"A guy was shot dead on Fifty-seventh Street between Madison and Fifth yesterday. Recent enough?"

"That's not exactly a cold case."

"No it isn't. But it's the most recent homicide we have. Want the skinny on the case, Jimmy?"

"Yes. Please."

"The vic was walking down Fifty-seventh Street a little after five at night, at the height of the rush hour, going toward Madison. A witness said a dirty old bum, looked like a homeless guy, tried to rob the vic. The vic refused to give the perp money, so the perp shot him dead. Right in front of Burberry. On the north side of Fifty-seventh Street."

I said, "You mentioned a witness. The witness say anything else?"

"Yes, he did. Let's see. Okay . . . the wit said he saw the whole thing, including the shooting. Says here the witness saw an old vagrant pull a revolver out of an overcoat pocket and shoot the vic in the neck. Says the vic died at the scene. The wit couldn't identify the shooter other than describing the shooter as old and who limped and used a cane. Let's see . . . says the witness thinks the cane had a silver handle, but he's not sure about that. The witness said by the time the cops got to the scene the killer was gone. Got lost in the five o'clock rush-hour crowd."

"What did the vic do?"

"I told you. He died."

"No. I mean, what did the victim do for a living?"

"The guy was Mafia. One of the Gimbino gang. It was most likely a mob hit. The hitter was probably a mob guy dressed like a bum. Then the hit man gets rid of the dirty coat and hat, stuffs them in a trash can, and disappears. We get a lot of that. Mob hits. One rat getting rid of another rat. That's why we don't try too hard to close those mob cases."

"No shit! The vic was a Mafia hit man?"

"Yes. Supposedly a good hit man, Jimmy. One of the best, they say."

"What was his name?"

"Lisciandro. Cicci 'The Nose' Lisciandro."

"I'm just curious, Eddie. Do you have any idea why he was called The Nose?'"

"Yeah, I know why. Because he used to whack his targets by hanging them up by their noses on meat hooks in meat lockers. Oh, and Jimmy."

"Yes?"

"The Deco murder/suicide case?"

"What about it?"

"It's now a murder case."

"You're kidding. What changed it, Eddie?"

"The medical examiner's report came in a couple of days ago. Should have called you. My fault. I apologize. Called old man Deco and told him. Anyway, Meyer met with Captain Bigatel, like I said, a couple of days ago and insisted the case be opened and changed to murder."

"How come?"

"Meyer told the captain he couldn't find any gunpowder on either of Deco's hands after a paraffin test. If Deco shot himself, he would have had some residue, gunpowder or something, on his hands, at least the hand he used to shoot himself. Meyer asked the Captain if the Deco case could at least be changed to a CUPPI."

"What's a . . . what did you say Meyer wanted to change it to?"

"A CUPPI. It means cause undetermined pending police investigation. Meyer said, and the boss eventually agreed with him, the case wasn't even a CUPPI. It was out-and-out murder. Hey, Jimmy."

"What?"

"Now you got yourself an honest-to-goodness murder on your hands."

3

When I went to sleep that evening, I had a dream.

In my dream it was a very warm afternoon. A short stumpy man with a fat, pockmarked face was walking along Fifty-seventh Street heading toward Madison Avenue. He was wearing a white wife beater underwear shirt with CICCI written across the front, and boxer shorts. There were tons of people on Fifty-seventh Street, but the stumpy man with the pockmarked face was the only one who was wearing just his underwear.

"I'm hot," he said, as he walked along the pavement. "I'm hot."

Suddenly an old man popped up right in front of the man with the pockmarked face. The old man was crippled and hunchbacked, and dressed in rags. He needed a cane to walk. Everybody ran away from the old man, except me. My legs wouldn't budge. The old man took out a huge gun from somewhere inside the pocket of his torn and tattered old overcoat and shot the pockmarked man in the face. The pockmarked man's face flew apart. Pieces of it were all over Fifty-seventh Street. Some parts of his face hung from lampposts. Some pieces were sticking to store windows. Some were on the pavement. I slipped on a piece of the pockmarked man's face and fell down. I skinned my knee because I was wearing short pants.

I watched as the old man ran down the street toward Madison Avenue. I got up from the pavement and ran after him. The old man ran like a youngster. Fast and nimble. I finally caught up with the old man and pulled him down.

He said, "Get your hands off of me, Notts."

The old vagrant was Arthur Deco Senior.

4

All the next day and into the night I sat on the porch thinking about my dream.

"Dinner's ready!" hollered Nettie from the dining room.

"I'm not hungry, Nettie."

"Well, come and keep me company."

That's all I did, this time, just kept Nettie company. I was too excited to eat.

"Did I tell you," I said, "the Deco case has now been ruled a full-fledged murder?"

"Yes. You told me last night. You okay, Jimmy?"

"I'm fine, Nettie. Just excited."

"I'm glad you're excited and not troubled."

Nettie ate for a bit, then said, "Why are you excited?"

"Last night I had this weird dream."

"Tell me about it."

When I finished telling Nettie my dream, she said, "Interesting."

Interesting? Interesting is another word for boring or not good. When you read a book that a friend wrote and it's a lousy book, you tell that person the book was "interesting."

"I'll tell you what's interesting, Nettie. I think that's the way the Deco case played out."

"Played out? I don't understand."

"What I'm trying to say is, I think that's how Junior was murdered."

"I still don't understand."

"Okay, I'll explain my dream to you again. Old man Deco hires a Mafia hit man to kill his son. In my dream, the hit man is the man with the pockmarked face. Then old man Deco dresses up like a bum with an old coat and hat and shoots the hit man on Fifty-seventh Street at the height of the five o'clock rush hour."

"Interesting."

"Nettie. Stop saying interesting."

"Okay. So tell me this. Why did Mr. Deco have to kill the hit man?"

"Because now Junior's case has been changed to murder. Old man Deco knows that. He also knows the hit man he hired to kill his son can blackmail him as often as he wants to. So Mr. Deco has to kill him."

"Why did he kill the Mafia man at five o'clock in the afternoon on Fifty-seventh Street?"

"It's the rush hour, Nettie. Old man Deco can get lost in the rush-hour crowds."

"If it's the rush hour, won't a lot of people be able to identify him?"

"Hopefully not."

"Okay. I have another question. What did Senior do with his hat and coat and gun?"

"The gun's easy," I said. "Senior took the gun back to Bowling Green on his private plane and got rid of it here. I don't know where. He could have tossed it into Drakes Creek, for all I know."

"And the hat and coat?" Nettie asked.

"The hat and coat? I don't know what he did with his hat and coat. Maybe he rented the hat and coat from a Salvation Army or a Goodwill store in New York and returned it. Or maybe he got rid of them here in Bowling Green. I don't know what he did with the hat and coat, Nettie."

"The Salvation Army only sells things, Jimmy, they don't rent."

"Then maybe Deco *bought* the coat at a Salvation Army store in New York and got rid of it somewhere else. Who cares?"

"Who cares? I'll tell you who cares. The police care. The Decos care. The Decos' lawyers care. Before you make any rash accusations based on your *dream*, you better have some concrete answers. *And* evidence. You don't go around pointing your finger at someone and call that person a murderer based on a dream, Jimmy. Good Lord."

Nettie was upset.

I knew the next thing I would tell my sister would upset her even more, but she had to know. "Nettie, this is my plan: I want everybody present at the Deco house. I want the Deco family and the Deco lawyers, the same crowd that was at the mansion when I was there last. I want to point my finger at Mr. Deco, and tell the mean old bastard how he had his son killed by a professional hit man. And then how the bastard killed the hit man who killed his son. And I want Lieutenant Eddie Roach and Detective Jackie Hallerhan there too, to act as witnesses. Maybe they should bring a tape recorder and record the confession."

"What about Eddie Cotton?" asked Nettie.

"Not him. He's innocent."

"All of a sudden Cotton's innocent. Well, Arthur Deco Senior's just as innocent as Cotton. I hate to bust your bubble, Jimmy, but you haven't a shred of evidence to back up what you're saying about Arthur

Deco Senior. No proof at all. Your entire theory is based on a *dream* you had, for God's sake. I'm not a lawyer, Jimmy, but in my mind you don't convict on dreams. You need evidence to convict someone of murder. You don't have a shred of evidence to convict Mr. Deco; no reliable witnesses, no proof, nothing. Not even a motive."

"I do so have a motive, Nettie. Senior can't stand gays and didn't want one in his family."

"If that's a motive, it's a very shaky one," said my sister. "And answer me this. If what you say is true, why did Senior hire you? To have you discover he's guilty of murder?"

"I don't know, Nettie. Maybe he *wants* to be found out. Listen, I've thought it all out again and again. I didn't sleep a wink last night. I stayed up all night writing notes, reams and reams of notes, putting all the pieces together. I did that all day today too. It all fits, Nettie. It's the only possible scenario."

"I didn't sleep a wink either. Jimmy, I—"

"Nettie, what if I get a confession?"

"From who?"

"From old man Deco."

"How?"

"By telling the Deco family what I told you. And maybe he'll say, *You're absolutely right, Mr. Netts.*"

"He's crazy if he says anything. Goodness, Jimmy, it's just your goofy, crazy mind at work. The Decos will laugh you out of their house *and* out of Bowling Green."

"Yeah, well, they laughed at General Billy Mitchell."

"Who the hell is General Billy Mitchell?"

"The guy who said you could land planes on ships at sea. Nobody believed him."

"This is murder, Jimmy. This is not about landing planes on

ships at sea. You can't mess around with murder. You need real facts behind you when you go accusing someone of murder.

"You haven't told me any facts, James." Nettie called me James when she was *really* upset. "None. Worse than that, you're . . . you're basing your entire prosecution, if that's what you call it, on what you *dreamed* happened."

"But I'm *sure* that's the way it was, Nettie. I'm absolutely sure."

"Jimmy, this isn't the way you do things as a private detective. You're playing. That's what you're doing. You're *playing* at being a private eye. You don't *play* private detective. You don't point your finger at somebody and accuse that person of murder. On a *hunch*. Or worse, on a dream. You. Just. Don't. Do. That."

My sister inhaled and exhaled, then continued.

"I keep telling you, you have to have evidence. You told me once you were positive Eddie Cotton did it. Now you're saying Arthur Deco Senior did it. You're saying the *father* murdered *his own son*! You can't walk into the Deco living room and point a finger at Mr. Arthur Deco Senior and say, *You killed your son!* You just can't. *Not unless you have proof positive.* These are important people in this town. The Decos *own* Bowling Green. You're dealing with murder here, Jimmy, and these are the Decos, with tons of money and high-powered lawyers."

"Barnsworth Bosley didn't look so high-powered to me."

"Jimmy, you're just being obstinate now. Believe me, the Decos will have your head."

"What can the Decos do to me, Nettie?"

"They can break you. They'll send you out of town tarred and feathered, and as broke as any human being could possibly be."

"I'm pretty broke as it is right now. How broke is broke?"

"These aren't nice people, Jimmy. These are mean, vindictive, and vengeful people. Arthur Deco Senior won't be happy until he's ruined you. And maybe me too. He has a lot of clout with the university's board of directors. Who knows what can happen to me? I'm sorry I talked you into being a private detective."

"I'm not."

"A couple of days ago you didn't want to be a private detective."

"I changed my mind. I'm excited now. I'll tell you this, Nettie. Being a private eye is a hell of a lot more fun than being a podiatrist."

"Good Lord, James."

Nettie was still *very* upset.

5

I telephoned Detectives Roach and Hallerhan in New York. I told them to come to Bowling Green as fast as they could.

"Yeah sure," said Jackie Hallerhan.

Jackie *would* say, "Yeah sure."

"Why?" asked Detective Roach, which in my opinion should have been the first question asked.

"I know who killed Art Deco," I said.

"Come on," said Eddie. I think I heard Jackie chuckle on the extension.

"I do know. And I need you to call the Decos and tell them to assemble again in the living room of their mansion. And to bring their lawyers."

"What am I going to say?"

"Tell them the case has been reopened and you have more questions to ask them. That certainly makes sense. Just get them all together again in the Deco living room. With their damn lawyers too. I need you to do this for me, Eddie. If they refuse, insist. It's important. The only way we'll get them all to come together again is if *you* ask them. They won't do shit for me."

"I don't know, Jimmy—"

"I also need you two to act as witnesses. I want you two to hear the guilty party's confession. I also need you to take down the murderer's statement."

"Wouldn't it be better getting you and them to come up to New York and do this in the station house?"

"That'll never happen, Lieutenant. They'll never do that in a million years. Not all of them and their lawyers. Never. The only place we'll get them all together is in the living room of the Deco mansion."

"What about Cotton?" asked Jackie Hallerhan on the extension.

"We don't need him. He's innocent."

"How do you know that?" asked Jackie.

"I just know, Jackie."

"Okay, Jimmy," said Detective Hallerhan, "stop fooling around. Who killed Art Deco?"

I hung up before they could tell me they weren't coming.

TEN

WHODUNIT?

I

Lieutenant Eddie Roach and Detective Jackie Hallerhan of the NYPD came to Bowling Green, Kentucky, two days after I called them. They were wearing the same suits they wore the first time we three met. Maybe they were the only suits they had. I wore a suit and tie too, which was a bit unusual for me.

Roach, Hallerhan, and I arrived at the Deco mansion just before noon. As we all got out of my car, Lieutenant Eddie Roach said to me, "Please make sure you have legitimate proof before you start pointing your finger at someone, or you can get us all in a whole lot of trouble. Keep that in mind, Jimmy."

"Like Eddie says," said Jackie Hallerhan, "think about that *before* you point your finger."

"I've thought about it," I said. "For days."

Then Eddie Roach gave me some new information concerning the Deco case. He told me the approximate time Arthur Deco Junior died. It was close to two-fifteen in the afternoon, give or take a few minutes. "The ME gave us that info about a week ago," he said. "I should have told you sooner."

"Shoulda, woulda, coulda. Anyway, it's not important to the confession I'm looking for, Eddie."

"Just keep it in mind," said Jackie Hallerhan.

"I will. Thanks."

I could tell by the assortment of cars that were parked in the circular drive that everyone had come. The three of us were escorted into the Deco living room by the speechless butler. The same cast of characters were there. Pudgy Barnsworth Bosley, the family attorney, dressed in crispy clean everything that was way too tight for him. Daughter Erica Bosley, still skinny, still without an ass and tits, still with her ugly prune-face. Miss Bosley wore a narrow black silk dress that did nothing to help her awful figure. She reminded me of Cruella de Vil.

The Deco family were all present and accounted for. It looked like everyone was sitting in exactly the same places where they had sat the last time I was there. Arthur Deco Senior, dressed in his stylish three-piece suit. His wife, Margaret Deco, wearing her red hair in a bun at the back of her head. Mrs. Deco held her hands in her lap, then stood to greet the three of us. She was her usual beautiful self. Seena Deco wore a sweater and skirt. She looked very pretty, at least to me.

The two married daughters were there. Mrs. Hattie Deco Strange, sitting slouched in her armchair in a suit and sensible shoes, looking furious as usual. And Mrs. Elizabeth Deco Brown, dumpy and fat, and very aware that she was dumpy and fat. Mrs. Brown sat up straight in her armchair in a far corner of the huge room, almost out of sight. She tried desperately to hide a yawn behind her hands. She looked like she usually looked, bored to death.

"So," said Arthur Deco Senior, "to what do we owe the pleasure of your company this time, Detectives?"

Senior intentionally ignored me as if I were trash on the carpet.

The lieutenant coughed, cleared his throat, and said, "As you know, your son's case has now been changed from a suicide to a murder."

"What took you so long?" said Senior, smirking.

"Certain new issues have made us change your son's death to a homocide," continued Lieutenant Roach. "For one thing, your son's gun, the one registered to him, was found in his right hand. We all know by now your son was left-handed. Also, and most importantly, the medical examiner informed us there wasn't any gunpowder residue on either of your son's hands. When someone shoots themselves, there is always some sort of gunpowder residue on one hand or the other. And . . . and . . ."

The lieutenant was stuck. He looked at Jackie. She froze, mouth agape. So I jumped in. It was my party, wasn't it? I had to get the show on the road. I took a deep breath and said, "I asked Lieutenant Roach and Detective Hallerhan to come to Bowling Green and act as witnesses."

"Witnesses?" said Mrs. Hattie Strange. "To what?"

"A confession of murder," I said.

My heart was pounding so loudly, I was sure everyone in the room could hear it. Damn if this wasn't exciting.

"I want Lieutenant Roach and Detective Hallerhan to witness the reaction of the murderer when I point the killer out."

"Coffee, anyone?" asked Margaret Deco.

"Mother!" snapped Senior. "This isn't the time to ask about coffee."

"How do you intend to get this confession?" asked Hattie Strange.

"By explaining to everyone what I have pieced together."

"What *you* pieced together?" Mrs. Strange snickered. "That should be good."

"Damn it, start!" growled Senior.

"Okay, I'll begin," I said, thinking, Seena will never talk to me again. I'll never get a chance to date her. Never.

I began.

"First of all, I checked a week ago with Lieutenant Roach on certain cold cases in New York. He didn't find any cold cases, but the lieutenant did find a new, unsolved one having to do with the killing of a mob guy between Fifth and Madison Avenues. Lieutenant Roach told me the mob guy that was shot and killed was a hit man for the Gimbino mob."

"What's the killing of some mobster on the streets of New York have to do with the death of my son?" snapped Arthur Deco Senior.

"You hired that mobster, Mr. Deco."

"I did? For what purpose?"

"To kill your son."

The only sound in the room was Margaret Deco gripping the arms of her chair as if she were on a roller-coaster ride. Seena Deco put her hand to her mouth. (Once again: Goodbye, Seena.) Hattie Strange sat bolt upright in her armchair. The two lawyers appeared confused. Mrs. Elizabeth Deco Brown still looked bored. She didn't seem to care if her father was a murderer or not.

"Why would I do something as stupid as that?" snorted Senior. "Hire a mob hit man to kill my son?"

"Because you didn't have the nerve to kill your son yourself."

Senior said, "I'd be very careful if I were you, Mr. Netts."

"Yes, be careful, Mr. Netts," said Barnsworth Bosley.

They scared me a little, but I went on anyway.

"You thought your son was a disgrace to the family, Mr. Deco. He was gay and you couldn't stand the thought that your gay son was part of the Deco family tree. You checked around in New York and found a mob contact who led you to this hit man. You hired the hit man to murder your son for you, didn't you, Mr. Deco?"

Mr. Barnsworth Bosley cleared his throat and said, "Don't answer that, Arthur." Then to me, "You have no evidence, Mr—"

"Let him finish, Barney," Senior said very quietly.

"Mr. Deco, that professional hit man was murdered in broad daylight during the five o'clock rush hour on Fifty-seventh Street between Fifth and Madison Avenues. The shooting took place at five-fifteen. A witness came forward and told the police he saw either a bent-over old homeless guy with a dirty overcoat and hat, and maybe using a cane with maybe a silver handle, walk up to the victim, shoot him dead, and walk away. The witness said the shooter got lost in the early evening crush of people."

"Do you have proof Daddy did any of this?" asked Mrs. Hattie Deco Strange.

"First let me finish," I said, my stomach sinking down to my scrotum. "The man Mr. Deco hired to murder his son makes Mr. Deco an accessory to murder. Why? Because Mr. Deco told the mob guy how to get into his son's building through the back way, told him about the apartment building's service elevator, told him Junior's apartment number and floor, even gave the killer his key to Junior's front door. Mr. Deco told the hit man where Junior kept his gun, and how to make the murder look like suicide.

"Lisciandro went up to Junior's apartment by the back way, entered the apartment, and killed Junior with his own gun. After Lisciandro shot Junior, the hit man put the gun in the wrong hand, compounded the mistake by forgetting that neither hand would have any gunpowder residue on it, left the apartment leaving the front door slightly open the same way he'd found it, then went down the service elevator to the street floor and out the rear entrance."

"I just bought Junior his own plane last March," said Arthur Deco Senior. "Why would I have my son murdered if I just bought him a brand-new plane?"

"Maybe that's *why* you bought Junior a brand-new plane," I said. "To deflect suspicion away from you as a possible suspect. Again, let me finish. So—"

"Mr. Netts," interrupted Hattie Strange, "your story is so ridiculous, it's pathetic."

"Fine. May I go on?"

At this point I *had* to go on. I didn't have any other alternatives.

"Okay, so the killing of Arthur Deco Junior was declared a suicide, not a murder, by the New York Police Department, and was taken off the precinct's books. You, Mr. Deco, thought you were home free.

"And then, to make you look even less guilty than you were, you did some research and found me, the newest private detective in Bowling Green, Kentucky. You did some further checking and discovered I was a podiatrist not that long ago and I most likely knew absolutely nothing about being a private detective. I was perfect. You would hire me and I would surely screw things up and never find out a damn thing.

"Now you could tell the world you believed your son was murdered, and that you even hired a private detective to find out who killed your son but the private detective didn't turn up a damn thing. By doing that you would come off as having gone down every avenue, but to no avail. More people would be thrown off the trail in the same way your buying Junior a new plane deflected suspicion.

"But then your son's case was reopened, and suddenly all your plans were screwed up. Now the only guy who could finger you, Mr. Deco, and say it was you who hired him to kill your son, which would send you directly to jail, was the hit man. Or just as bad, he could blackmail you for the rest of your life. You had to get rid of him too. So you contacted Lisciandro and told him to meet you on Fifty-seventh Street, between Fifth and Madison Avenues in front of Burberry at five-fifteen in the evening. Maybe you said you'd have a nice bonus for him, or another job. How you got him there was unimportant, as long as you got him there.

"When you saw Lisciandro come walking down Fifty-seventh Street, you went up to him dressed like an old homeless guy wearing a dirty old hat and overcoat, put a gun under his neck, and blew him away. Then you got lost in the five-fifteen rush-hour crowd."

I stopped momentarily. There was a deafening silence in the spacious room. I happened to notice Mrs. Deco had her fist in her mouth. I went on.

"You killed the hit man yourself, Mr. Deco, the way I just described it. You knew that Friday night at five-fifteen Fifty-seventh Street between Fifth and Madison Avenues would be jammed with people going home. It was a good time to shoot someone and get lost. Smart thinking, sir. And after you shot the hit man, after you got lost in the rush-hour crowd, you got rid of the dirty old coat and hat. Threw it in a trash can, I suppose. The big topcoat you were wearing covered the three-piece suit you usually wear. You looked like a different man as soon as you got rid of your costume. You looked like the patrician patriarch you are. Not a vagrant.

"You took the gun back to Bowling Green with you on your private plane. Eventually you got rid of it too. God knows where. Maybe you tossed the gun into Drakes Creek. Now not only are you an accessory to a murder, Mr. Deco, but you are also a murderer.

First you hired Cicci 'The Nose' Lisciandro to kill your son, then you killed him."

I was finished. There was a hush in the living room. The hush seemed to go forever. It was unnerving. I had obviously failed. I had screwed up just like Nettie said I would. My good friends, the two detectives, would now be in serious trouble because of me. And because of me, Nettie would probably lose her job at Western. God knows what horrible fate was in store for me.

And then Mr. Deco said, "You're absolutely right, Mr. Netts. I killed that man just like you said I did."

ELEVEN

And Then What Happened?

I

Mrs. Hattie Deco Strange said, "Oh, for God's sake, Daddy, you're so full of soup it's coming out your ears. You could no more kill anybody than . . . than . . . Lizzie."

I practically shouted, "Your father just confessed, Mrs. Strange."

"Sure. You know why, Mr. Netts? *To protect me*. Daddy saw me enter Junior's apartment building. He was half a block away, up Park Avenue. You were, weren't you, Daddy?"

Mr. Deco didn't answer.

"Well, he was. My father saw me walk into Junior's apartment building, Mr. Netts. Daddy figured I was there to kill my brother. You see, Mr. Netts, I told my daddy I was going to shoot my brother. Or intimated as much. I told him a couple of days earlier at my parents' house. I went there to have breakfast with Daddy. He eats by himself at seven sharp every morning. I wanted to talk to him, just the two of us. I told my father that morning I was going to shoot Junior. Or intimated as much. Daddy thought I wasn't serious. In the end I convinced Daddy I only wanted to go shopping in New York. I was delighted Daddy let me come with him on his private plane because then I could carry my husband's revolver in my purse and not have to worry about security."

"I suggest you not say anything else, Hattie," said Cruella de Vil.

"Oh, for God's sake, be quiet, Erica. As I was saying, we flew up about noon, Daddy and me. Late that afternoon, Daddy saw me enter Junior's building and thought I was on my way up to my brother's apartment to shoot him. That's what you thought, Daddy, now, wasn't it? I *know* that's what Daddy thought, Detective. No, my father couldn't kill a soul and I will not let him be convicted of something he did not do. Daddy's all bluster, Detective. I killed my brother."

"*You* killed your brother?" said Lieutenant Eddie Roach, getting out of his armchair and walking to the center of the room. He faced Mrs. Strange. "And it's Lieutenant, Mrs. Strange."

"Yes, I did, *Lieutenant*," said Hattie, smiling.

"She did not," said Senior.

Lieutenant Roach turned around to face Mr. Deco.

"I told you, Lieutenant, I did," said Senior. "I hired that Italian hit man, Leechiano, whatever his name is . . . was . . . to do it, just as Mr. Netts said I did. Then I killed him before he could blackmail me, again exactly as Mr. Netts described. I'm the one. I will write out a statement confessing to the murder of the man I hired to kill my son."

Lieutenant Roach turned his back on Mr. Deco and said, "Mrs. Strange, how did you kill your brother?"

Hattie brightened. "I walked into Junior's build—"

"About what time?" interrupted an interested Lieutenant Roach.

"Excuse me, *Lieutenant*?"

"About what time did you walk into your brother's building?"

"About four in the afternoon. I had done some shopping before I went to his place. I had been to Bergie's—"

"Bergie's?" said Lieutenant Roach.

"Bergdorf Goodman's, for God's sake," explained Hattie Strange, annoyed. "And then I went to Hermès to exchange something. I finished those chores around three-thirty in the afternoon. *Then* I walked over to—"

"Excuse me, Mrs. Strange," said Lieutenant Roach, "about what time were you in Bergdorf Goodman's and Hermès, and do you have any witnesses that can confirm you were in those stores when you say you were?"

"Goodness, *Lieutenant,* are you ever going to let me finish my confession?" said Hattie Strange. "Yes, the salesgirls who waited on me will remember me and the time I was there. I always make such a fuss about *everything.*" Mrs. Strange giggled.

"Go on, Mrs. Strange," said Roach.

"I insist that you do *not* go on, Hattie," said Barnsworth Bosley.

"I walked over to Junior's building," said Hattie Strange, ignoring the family lawyer. "I asked the concierge to tell my brother I had come to see him. The concierge told me the door was already open. He mentioned something about Junior calling down and saying the door would be open, that he might be in the shower or something. The message was for his queer roommate, I suppose. So I took the elevator up to Junior's floor."

"Hattie," Mrs. Deco said, her voice practically a whisper, "please. It's all a nightmare as it is."

"Well, he is a queer, Mother. We all know that. Anyway, the door was open just like the concierge said it would be, so I just walked in. My brother was doing something in the living room. I said hello. We hugged. I told Junior I had to go to the bathroom, badly. He said, 'You know where it is,' and I . . . and I . . . I walked into his bedroom. I knew where Junior kept his gun. He showed me where he kept it months ago. I . . . uh . . . I decided to use his gun and not my husband's. I went to where he said it would be and—"

"Where *did* he keep his gun, Mrs. Strange?" asked Detective Hallerhan.

"In a bedside table drawer. On the right side, in the top drawer. He said he kept it there because he always slept on the right side of the bed."

"Facing the bed or lying in the bed?" asked Hallerhan.

"Lying in the bed. If you were *facing* the bed, standing at the foot of Junior's bed, the gun would have been in the table drawer on the left side of the bed."

"Thank you, Mrs. Strange," said Detective Hallerhan.

"Go on," said Lieutenant Roach.

"Where was I?" asked Hattie Deco Strange. "Oh, yes, my brother was doing something in the living room and I went into his bedroom to go to the bathroom. I didn't go to the bathroom. I went to the bedside table and got his gun. I went back to the living room and shot Junior in the head."

Mrs. Deco said, "Oh, my God."

"Sorry, Mother. After my brother was lying on the floor, I put the gun in his right hand. I forgot my brother was left-handed. At that point I wasn't thinking clearly. I was a wee bit nervous and jumpy, I guess. Then I left the building. In a hurry. I took a cab to Teterboro Airport and met my father."

"Why did you kill your brother, Mrs. Strange?" asked Lieutenant Roach.

"Because I hated the little pervert. Because he was a sick queer. They don't call them queers for nothing. They are all sick and perverted and diseased and—"

"Okay, Mrs. Strange," said the lieutenant. "By the way, did you wipe your fingerprints off the bed table drawer and the gun?"

"I . . . uh . . . yes," said Hattie Strange. "Yes, I did. With my handkerchief."

Well, Jimmy, I thought, there goes your damn dream theory. Old man Deco's innocent as the driven snow.

And then someone shouted, "Excuse me!"

Everyone looked over to where frumpy Mrs. Elizabeth Deco Brown was standing.

"I killed Junior," she said quietly, hugging herself and looking at her shoes.

2

"Damn it, Elizabeth, be quiet and sit down," said Arthur Deco Senior with great disgust.

"I did kill Junior, Daddy. I *swear* I did. By everything that's holy." Then, turning to Lieutenant Roach, Lizzie Deco Brown said, "I killed Junior." She paused and said, "Lieutenant?"

"Yes, Mrs. Brown?"

"My father is protecting my sister Hattie, and Hattie is trying her best to protect our father. But they are both wasting their time."

"Why is that?" asked the lieutenant.

"You know damn well why, Lieutenant," said Lizzie angrily. "I just told you why. I killed my brother. I shot him in the head and killed him. That's why they're wasting their time."

None of the Deco family, nor their lawyers, made a sound. They were all stunned that Lizzie was saying anything, let alone what she was saying.

"Please sit down and tell us about it, Mrs. Brown," said a calm Lieutenant Eddie Roach. He walked over to where Lizzie was standing and watched her sit down.

"Well," said Lizzie, "I will be extremely happy to get this off my chest. It's been a terrible weight to bear. Okay, here goes. I flew up to New York from Nashville on July twelfth, at seven-ten in the morning on American Airlines Flight 1088, if I remember correctly. I arrived at La Guardia about ten-thirty that morning. I took a taxi into the city, got there close to eleven, and wasted about an hour and a half doing nothing."

"How?" asked Lieutenant Roach.

"Excuse me?" said Lizzie Deco Brown.

"How did you waste an hour and a half, Mrs. Brown?"

"I walked up and down Fifth Avenue and Madison Avenue, mostly, looking in store windows. I stopped in coffee shops for coffee twice. Things like that."

"Go on, please," said Lieutenant Roach.

"I did that until about one-thirty. Then I headed over to Junior's place. I walked. I got there a few minutes after two o'clock. There were a bunch of people outside standing in front of the revolving door. I went into the building through a side door. The doorman didn't notice me. I don't think. Same thing happened when I walked past the concierge's desk. He was surrounded by people too. I don't think he noticed me either. I took the elevator to Art's floor, walked down the hall, and knocked, but as I knocked, the door opened up on its own. I guessed Art had left it open for someone. When I walked into Art's apartment it was exactly two-ten in the afternoon."

"How did you know it was *exactly* two-ten?" asked Lieutenant Roach.

"I looked at the clock on Art's mantel. I gave my brother that clock. I bought the clock for him as a birthday present. At Tiffany. The clock is engraved from me to him. They have a really nice selection of clocks at Tiffany. I always look at that clock when I visit Junior."

"Go on, Mrs. Brown," urged Detective Roach.

"Junior once told me his housekeeper, her name is Damaris, always left his apartment at two in the afternoon. I remembered that. That's why I made sure to arrive at my brother's place after two in the afternoon. When I walked into Junior's living room I could hear the shower running. I presumed my brother was taking a shower. Real smart, right?" Lizzie allowed a smile to cross her face. "I went into Junior's bedroom and found his gun. He showed me where he put it ages ago. In the bedside table drawer. Just as Hattie explained. I suppose Junior showed Hattie where he kept his gun too.

"I took the gun, went back into the living room, sat down, and waited. I pushed the gun down between the chair's pillow and the armrest. My brother finally walked into the living room. His hair was wet. He hadn't dried his hair yet. He looked cute and seemed actually glad to see me. For a moment I had second thoughts. Junior wore a black T-shirt, jeans, no belt, and Birkenstocks. He turned his back on me and walked over to his living room window. The window faces Central Park. It's a really beautiful view. My brother looked out of his living room window down to the street below. He seemed to be looking for someone. Then he turned back to talk to me. That's when I got up, walked across the room, hiding the gun behind my back. I arrived at his right side.

"My brother said, 'What have you behind your back, Lizzie? A present for me?'"

"That's when I shot him."

Mrs. Margaret Deco moaned aloud, and then started to quietly cry. Arthur Deco Senior moved to her couch and put his arm around his wife.

Everyone in that room knew Lizzie Deco Brown was telling the truth.

"When I shot Junior he just dropped to the floor," said Lizzie. "When he landed on the floor, a Birkenstock fell off his right foot. I remember the Birkenstock lying beside his bare left foot. I have no idea why I remember that, I just do.

"I put the gun in Junior's right hand," said Mrs. Elizabeth Deco Brown. "I wanted to make the murder appear to be a suicide."

"Why was that?" asked the lieutenant.

"I really don't know," answered Lizzie Deco Brown.

"Did you know your brother was left-handed?" asked Roach.

"Yes, I did. I don't know why I put the gun in Junior's right hand. Just plain stupid, I guess."

"Go on," said the lieutenant.

"Then I went into the kitchen, got a dish towel, and went back to the bedroom. I wiped around the knob of the bed table drawer, and anything else I might have touched in Junior's bedroom. Then I went to the living room and did the same with the gun. When I finished wiping my fingerprints off the gun, I put it back in Junior's right hand, forgetting once again my brother was left-handed, making the same mistake a second time. How dumb can you get?

"Then I went to the front door and wiped the doorknob on the outside of the door, and all around it. I wiped the knob on the inside and around it too. I put the dish towel in my purse. When I walked out of Junior's apartment I looked at the clock on Junior's mantel again. The time was exactly two-twenty. I left the door open farther than it was when I found it. I was in a hurry.

"I took the freight elevator down to the ground floor and went out of the building using the back door. Art showed me the back way out once when I visited him. He said then that he was trying to avoid someone in the lobby. I thought I better go that way. I might not be as lucky going out of the building as I was coming in, as far as being seen was concerned. I took a taxi back to La Guardia and caught the first plane to Nashville. I had to go by way of Chicago."

"Why did you have to go to Nashville by way of Chicago?" asked Detective Hallerhan.

"Because I missed the last flight to Nashville. I drove my car to Bowling Green. I got home very late. And that's it."

Lizzie sighed and leaned back in her armchair.

You could cut the silence with a knife, until Lieutenant Eddie Roach said, "Lizzie, why did you kill your brother? Because he was gay?"

"Oh, no. Not at all. Personally I couldn't care less that Junior was gay."

"Then why did you murder him?" asked Jackie Hallerhan.

"To make my father proud of me." she said "My father's never been proud of me my entire life. I knew if I killed my gay brother, my homophobic father would be proud of me."

"But why did you wait so long to confess?" asked Lieutenant Roach. "If you murdered your brother for your father's approval, why didn't you tell your father right away?"

"Well, Lieutenant Roach, first of all I didn't want to go to jail. When y'all declared my brother's death a suicide, it began to look as though I wouldn't go to jail. I thought I'd just keep it to myself for a while, and tell Daddy sometime in the future. But when you changed my brother's death to murder, then it became a different story. I knew you would be back questioning us. I figured I would tell you then."

"I see," said Eddie Roach.

"And Lieutenant?"

"What, Mrs. Brown?"

"Daddy wouldn't have believed me no matter when I told him."

3

A month later, in September, I saw Seena Deco.

I was walking across the square from my office. I was going to get a cup of coffee. Seena was sitting on a bench in the town square. She was wearing a raincoat, though it hadn't been raining.

"How are you, Seena?" I asked.

"I'm fine, and you?"

"Good, thank you." I screwed up all my courage and said, "May I sit for a minute?"

"Sure, please do," she said, moving over. I sat down next to Seena. She offered me a weak smile.

"I'm sorry about everything that happened, Seena . . . I mean . . ."

"I know. I read the letter you sent to my mother. So what have you been doing with yourself, Jimmy, since Lizzie's confession?"

"Not much, Seena. The fallout of your family's situation has really shaken me to the core. I'm still not over it. I mean, the damage I did . . ." I shook my head from side to side.

"You are not going to stop being a private detective, are you?"

"I don't know, Seena. I . . . I don't know."

There was silence.

"How's your family?" I asked.

"My mother seems to be the one who took all of this the hardest. The loss of one child killed by another, that's rough. Mother hasn't been as well as she should be. She's aged a lot, poor thing. She's also been very depressed, and that's not like her.

"My sister Hattie despises all the notoriety the murder has caused our family. She thinks the worst of all worlds has landed squarely on her shoulders. She is convinced she and her husband and her kids are being shunned because of Junior's being gay. She's wrong, but that's what she thinks. Oh, and she swears she's going to kill you."

I laughed, sort of.

"My father's not well either. His health has deteriorated too since all of this nonsense began. He's become a sick man. And Lizzie's her usual vacant self. She has no idea, I don't think, of the damage she has caused our entire family, all for Father's approval. The family lawyers are constantly working on her case. They may plead temporary insanity. Lizzie doesn't seem to mind that she may go to prison or a mental hospital for years and years if certain judgments go against her. My sister is totally without feelings. She will never change. Even if she goes to prison, she will never change."

"And you?"

"Me?" Seena Deco thought about that question for a bit, then answered, "Constantly bummed, I guess you would say. I moved out of our house. I couldn't take it there for another minute. I bought my own home and moved into it. It is a very nice house on Drakes Creek. It has a beautiful weeping willow tree on the front lawn."

"I love weeping willow trees."

"I do too. I think I better get going, Jimmy. I have someone meeting me at my house to give me a piano lesson. I'm learning how to play the piano now. Takes my mind off all the bad things, for a little while at least. My car is parked over there, across from the Capital Arts Center. Remember, Jimmy, what's happened to my family is not your fault. You were only doing what you were hired to do by my father. I just wonder why my father hired you in the first place."

"I wonder about that too," I said. "I guess since he didn't kill Junior, as I unfortunately believed he did, he simply wanted to find out who did. He said over and over again that your brother didn't have the guts to kill himself, that Junior was murdered, and he was right."

"My brother would *never* take his own life. Guts never entered into it. I'm sure of that."

And then I suddenly said, "Seena, would you ever consider having dinner with me?"

"Not in town," she answered quickly. "It's not that I don't want to be seen with you, Jimmy. It's just that I don't want to be seen in public, period. Constantly answering people's questions. Seeing them staring at me, then quickly looking away. But I'll be happy to make you dinner some night at my place, Jimmy, but only if you promise me something."

"Anything, Seena."

"Will you promise to tell me how that absurd scenario got in your head? You know, the one about Daddy dressing up like a homeless vagrant and killing that mobster on Fifty-seventh Street."

"That's a deal. I promise I'll tell you. May I have your address and phone number?"

Seena Deco wrote her address and phone number on a piece of paper she found in her purse.

I took the piece of paper, stuffed it in my pocket, thanked Seena for her address, and told her it was really good seeing her again. She stood. We shook hands. Then Seena turned and walked toward her automobile, and I walked across the square for my coffee.

Acknowledgments

I would like to thank the following people for their help: My editor Sarah Hochman, my police advisor Detective Lieutenant Michael J. Murphy of the NYPD, my agent Jennifer Lyons, and my wife, Mary Barris.